> So many rumors flew around the
> school about Nick that you never
> knew what was true and what wasn't.

A different girl every night. Cutting classes. Detention at least three times a week.

A different girl every night. I had no doubt.

Nick Adriano might be every girl's dream at Kennedy High, but he'd never been mine. Yeah, he was amazing looking. But whatever it was that guys like Nick Adriano talked about, I was sure it wasn't anything that I talked about. I mean, what would we possibly have to say to each other? I doubted that Nick was into nuclear fusion.

What did guys like Nick talk about? *Did* they talk?

"It occurred to me," Nick suddenly murmured in a low voice as if he feared someone other than me might hear him, "that you probably didn't realize I was serious about us going to the dance together."

Huh? So he *had been* serious?

His. Hers. Theirs.

Nick & the Nerd

RACHEL HAWTHORNE

BANTAM BOOKS
NEW YORK · TORONTO · LONDON · SYDNEY · AUCKLAND

RL: 6, AGES 012 AND UP

NICK & THE NERD
A Bantam Book / June 2001

Cover photography by Barry Marcus

*Copyright © 2001 by 17th Street Productions,
an Alloy Online, Inc. company, and Jan Nowasky.
Cover copyright © 2001 by 17th Street Productions,
an Alloy Online, Inc. company.*

*Produced by 17th Street Productions,
an Alloy Online, Inc. company.
151 West 26th Street
New York, NY 10001.*

ISBN: 0-553-49372-8

Visit us on the Web! www.randomhouse.com/teens

Published simultaneously in the United States and Canada

*Bantam Books is an imprint of Random House Children's Books, a
division of Random House, Inc. BANTAM BOOKS and the rooster
colophon are registered trademarks of Random House, Inc. Bantam Books,
1540 Broadway, New York, New York 10036.*

PRINTED IN THE UNITED STATES OF AMERICA

OPM   0 9 8 7 6 5 4 3 2 1

To Isabelle, Charlotte, and Eliza

One

Nick

He who accepts a dare risks much.
—Mama Ling

CAFETERIA FOOD WAS the most uncool thing on the planet. Half the time I wasn't even sure what I was moving around on the tray. But food wasn't what drew me to the cafeteria at Kennedy High every lunch period. It was my loyalty to my friends, Jared Fletch and Steve Cochran, who were sitting across from me, attacking their fries.

Steve had recently had his off-campus lunch privilege suspended because he'd parked in the Teacher of the Year's reserved slot. I personally thought the punishment was a little harsh. After all, the teacher had been out sick that day and wasn't even using the space.

But, as my father had sternly pointed out, order within an institution had to be maintained. My dad is an ex-marine. Well, people who don't know any better refer to him that way, but as my father had drilled into me from the moment I'd been able to hold my hand in a salute, there was no such thing as an ex-marine. A marine was a marine was a marine.

Anyway, thanks to Steve using the teacher's spot, we were slumming in the cafeteria—and would be for an entire month.

"Hey, Nick, don't look so bummed," Steve told me, moving his shaggy brown hair out of his green eyes so he could see his fries, which were totally soggy. Some of 'em were even still frozen in the middle. "We only have three weeks left of eating in the dungeon."

I shoved my tray aside, thinking that eating that stuff could make a person seriously ill. "I'm not bummed. Just thinking," I said, which was true. "I can't decide who to ask to the dance on Saturday."

Kennedy High's semiformal was all anyone was talking about these days.

"Dude, just snap your fingers at the next girl you pass," Jared suggested before he shoved something that looked like orange worms, but was probably macaroni and cheese, into his mouth.

I rolled my eyes and responded half jokingly, "I can't choose lightly. The girl who goes to the dance with me will make a statement about my taste in women."

More for me than my fellow classmates. I didn't want to take just any girl to the dance. And okay,

I'm just gonna say this outright even if you think I'm a totally conceited jerk. Any girl I'd ask would say yes. *Any* girl.

I'm serious. Girls at Kennedy High like me. Really *like* me. I felt their eyes follow me wherever I went. Watching, waiting for me to dart a glance their way. And when I did—bam! They always gave me a hundred-megawatt smile like I'd just flipped the switch that provided the electricity that ran through their hearts.

Nick Adriano, aka me, god of Kennedy. It was crazy.

It had been this way for as long as I could remember. The reason mostly had to do with the way I looked—an "Italian Adonis," a lot of the girls said—and the way I acted, like I absolutely didn't care one way or the other about anything or anyone. It was an absolute turn-on for babes, and it earned me the admiration of every guy who darkened the halls of Kennedy High.

Why was it so cool to act like you didn't care about anyone or anything? I didn't get it. But it had worked for me for so long that I sorta just adopted it as me a long time ago. I wouldn't even know how to be any different. Anyway, why would I want to be? Being this way got me everything a guy in high school could need.

Except the girl of my dreams. Not that I knew who that was. So who was I supposed to ask to the dance? It was Monday, and the dance was this Saturday. I had to get moving.

The problem was that I really couldn't decide. There wasn't a girl at Kennedy with whom I truly wanted to spend a whole evening. Again, I don't mean to sound like a jerk, but I couldn't drum up enough enthusiasm about someone who was into me just because she thought I was cool or good-looking.

As my buds were stuffing their faces with inedible food, I looked around the caf and found some girls checking me out and some totally staring, but I was very aware that no one really knew *me*. I mean, they all knew the outer yeah-I've-got-attitude Nick, but no one knew the guy underneath that layer of attitude. And I thought, hoped, that guy was a pretty good person.

But like I said, no one knew him. And the truth was that sometimes I wasn't even sure I did either. You know?

"Well, you'd better make up your mind fast, buddy," Steve said. "A lot of guys are bummed out about the fact that the hottest girls are holding themselves open just in case you ask them. Why do you think Jar and I are going stag?"

Oh, man. Why did all those girls want to go to the dance with me? So they could walk in with a guy everyone thought was cool and popular? How did they even know they'd like me once they spent five minutes in my supposedly desirable presence?

"You know what, man?" I began. "I wish I could ask some geek who doesn't even know who I am."

"Excuse me?" Jared said, raking his hand through

his thick, blond hair, his dark blue eyes wide on me. "Why would a geek not know who you are? Everyone knows who you are."

"Yeah, I guess." I stared at my plate. Too bad. It would be truly cool to spend time with a girl who didn't know that I ruled Kennedy High, someone who saw something beyond the attitude, looks, and popularity. Someone who wasn't interested in any of that stuff, like the kind of girls who actually got into dissecting frogs or their math homework. I'd never even spoken to a girl like that before. And that type of girl didn't even notice guys, right? I mean, they were into reading *The Canterbury Tales* (which I was struggling through in English) and entering science fairs. Guys and parties weren't their thing. That's the kind of girl I wanted to take to the dance. Someone who didn't even know I was alive, someone who'd actually want to know what I thought about stuff.

"Anyway, who are you kidding?" Steve said, polishing off his Coke. "No way would you ask a geekizoid to the dance."

"Yeah," Jared agreed, popping a fry into his mouth. "Even *you* care about what people think. You'd never ask some science-fair nerd."

Was that true?

I didn't think so. But was it?

Nah. Definitely not true. "I don't care what *anyone* thinks," I insisted.

Jared and Steve both snorted.

"I don't," I repeated. "Why would I? My reputation

5

around here would let me get away with just about anything."

Sometimes I really believed that. My friends did too, apparently, because they nodded.

"If I asked the geekiest, nerdiest, least-cool girl in this school," I added, "I'll bet everyone would think it was my detention or something or that I was doing something charitable. So it doesn't even matter that I don't care what people think because they'd think *better* of me anyway. But I don't care what people think, so this whole conversation is stupid." I slurped my Coke and looked around the caf to let them know the subject was closed.

My friends eyed me, then each other, then looked back to me with evil smiles.

Evil smiles meant trouble.

"Prove it," Jared challenged, leaning forward as if he was on the verge of imparting some wisdom that would better my life. "*Prove* you don't care what people think. I dare you to take the geekiest girl at Kennedy High to the dance."

I raised an eyebrow. "You *dare* me? What is this, second grade? Gimme a break, guys."

"*We* dare you," Steve put in.

I shook my head and laughed, then stole the one crisp fry off Jared's plate.

Jared grabbed my wrist. "So? Do you accept or not?"

I shook my wrist free and ate the fry. "Don't tell me you're serious?"

They both folded their arms across their chests

and looked at me. "Oh, we're serious," Steve said, his green eyes way too gleeful. "We dare you to ask a geek to the semiformal. There. You've been dared. Will you accept and admit that you care what people around here think?"

There was no way I couldn't accept. First of all, I *didn't* care what people thought. Second, asking a geekette to the dance would be a totally cool thing to do, a nice thing to do. A geek would no doubt be utterly and completely grateful. I'd be giving her a few hours in the inner circle, entry into the crowd she'd never even be permitted to walk next to in the hallway.

Just like in *The Nutty Professor.* Eddie Murphy had been given a chance to know what it was to be a babe magnet. So for one night I would make some geekizoid's secret fantasy come true. If geeks even *had* fantasies—other than winning the Westinghouse.

Okay, so the whole idea bordered on being a little mean-spirited. All right, it was a lot mean-spirited. But my friends had made me wonder about something: Was I really above my reputation? Was I cool enough not to care what people thought by asking a totally not-hot girl to the dance? Not even a not-hot girl. A *total nerd.*

Yeah. Of course, I was cool enough. Absolutely. Right?

Jared and Steve raised their eyebrows because I seemed to be stalling—which I was. I was not in the habit of lightly accepting dares. I had a reputation to maintain.

"So you *do* care what people think," Steve concluded, smirking. "Very uncool."

"I *don't* care what anyone thinks," I said for the hundredth time.

"Then take the dare," Jared challenged me.

I sighed. "All right, I will. Besides, accepting the dare will save me the hassle of deciding which girl to ask." Brilliant rationale. "So pick her out for me, and I'll ask her."

Putting their heads together, they whispered conspiratorially. I could see their gazes darting around the cafeteria like a fly at a picnic unable to decide which dessert to land on.

I began to relax. I mean, how awful could this be? It wasn't as if we had a female version of the hunchback of Notre Dame walking the halls of our school. Did we? Oh God. Maybe I'd just never noticed her before. I mean, why would I?

"You have to ask her *publicly,*" Jared said. "Everyone has to know that you're taking the geek to the dance."

I shrugged nonchalantly, trying not to care, wondering why I had to *try.* I had accepted the dare because I *didn't* care. It was an easy dare. "No problem."

A triumphant gleam sparkled in Jared's blue eyes. He looked at Steve. Steve nodded. My stomach clenched as my mind heard this thundering drumroll. I held my breath, waiting for the opening of the envelope. . . .

"Edie Dalton," Jared announced with a jubilant grin.

Edie Dalton? My jaw dropped.

They totally cracked up, cackling so hard that I thought they might actually start holding their stomachs and rolling on the floor. Jared knocked his fist against Steve's. They had succeeded in totally bumming me out with their choice. I mean, really, could they have picked anyone worse?

When I thought of Edie, I had a vision of an alien with a really huge brain—like the ones in old black-and-white sci-fi movies. Not that Edie had a funny-looking head. It was just that she was beyond supersmart. I didn't know how she managed to cram all that intelligence into her head. She was enrolled in honors classes. When she was a freshman, she'd probably been disappointed that we didn't have honors phys ed. In Edie's vocabulary *cool* only applied to temperature, not attitude.

"She's over there." Jared chortled, pointing behind me.

Hesitantly I glanced over my shoulder and instantly spotted Edie. She was the queen of shy. She sat at a table alone, writing in a notebook while she ate. Only an absolute geek would do schoolwork during lunch. She wore thick glasses. I knew I shouldn't judge the glasses harshly. After all, we didn't have much say in how good our vision was, but those clothes . . . dork city. Baggy, loose fitting. Her body probably got lost in them. Of course, if it did, it could find its way back easily enough because the bright yellow and green would serve as a homing beacon.

For someone who usually blended in with the lockers, today she stood out like a neon sign. Probably the reason she'd captured Jared and Steve's attention. Her good fortune was my bad luck.

Ah, man, I figured she'd come close to fainting when I asked her out. Girls like her probably didn't even dare to dream about guys at all. Did I sound like a jerk? I just figured that's the way it was. Getting her to accept would be a breeze. The hard part, however, would be pretending that I wasn't totally embarrassed to ask her to be my date.

Oops. *Embarrassed.* Did that mean that I *did* care what people thought or that I cared what *I* thought? I wasn't exactly sure. Somewhere between the time the dare had been issued and the choice of "geek" made, my thought processes had gotten convoluted.

But a dare was a dare, and it would be infinitely more embarrassing to back out.

"Go on, go ask her," Jared goaded.

I turned back around and faced them. Suddenly my lunch looked considerably more appetizing than fulfilling the dare. "What's the rush? No one else will ask her, and she definitely won't say no."

Steve eyed me, his blue eyes twinkling. "You care what people think. You can't deal with asking her in front of everybody."

I pointed at him with a french fry. "I've already told you that I *don't.*"

"Then ask her now," Jared added.

Ask her now. Sure.

I stood up. I felt eyes on me as usual. For once it would be great if no one noticed *I* existed, if no one followed my every move. Every girl in the caf would see me go up to Edie Dalton and ask her to the dance. Every girl!

Oh, man.

A few months ago the local news station did some feature about teenagers and who they'd want to be stranded with on a desert island. A lot of girls said me, which I found pretty embarrassing, but my dad got a kick out of it. Edie's answer had been Mother Teresa. I only remember that because my dad had commented on it. He'd said that was a good and surprising answer for a teenage girl.

Mother Teresa.

Not Freddie Prinze, Jr., or Justin Timberlake, or even yours truly, Nick Adriano. She wanted to be stranded with a person who had dedicated her life to good deeds. Not that her choice was a bad one. It's just that I figured if you were asked a fantasy question, you ought to provide a fantasy answer. Then again, Mother Teresa had passed away, so I guess it would be fantasy.

And here I was, about to gift her with one amazing fantasy come to life: an actual date with Nick Adriano.

I had to get over myself.

I stopped in front of Edie's table just as she was standing. There were a few people sitting at the other end, but otherwise she'd clearly eaten lunch by herself. I don't think I'd ever done that.

I looked her over. Had I ever noticed how tiny she was? Did the top of her head reach my shoulder? Not that it mattered. The one thing Steve and Jared hadn't stipulated, thank goodness, was that I had to dance a slow dance with her. If I danced with her at all, it would be something fast.

As if she were a puppet whose string had suddenly gotten yanked, she jerked. Behind the thick lenses of her glasses she blinked her dark, almond-shaped eyes rapidly as if she'd just noticed me standing there and wondered where I'd come from.

I searched my brain for something to say to a girl like her. I never initiated conversation with girls. I just responded to it when the mood struck. Most girls were content just to ramble on whether I commented or not.

This was so totally weird to stand before a girl who wasn't smiling brightly and looking around for some sort of support before her legs gave out beneath her. I cleared my throat. Just ask the question. Get it over with. I turned around and saw Jared and Steve gawking at me, their hands trained to their ears to exaggerate that they were listening. I turned back around. Edie wasn't even looking at me. She was cleaning crumbs off the table onto the tray. Only a total geekizoid would clean up after herself.

"Edie?" I began.

She glanced at me with a confused expression, then returned her attention to the crumbs, which she was sliding onto her tray with the help of the side of her hand.

Huh? Crumbs were more interesting than finding out what I, Nick Adriano, could possibly want?

I cleared my throat. "Um, Edie, I've decided to take you to the dance on Saturday."

She froze for a second. "Sorry," she said, her eyes still on the crumbs. "But, uh, thanks." And then she turned and walked away.

I stared stupidly at her quickly retreating back. *Sorry?* Had I heard her right? How could she possibly say no? It didn't make any sense.

Sorry, but thanks.

I didn't get it. Did she mean she wasn't interested in the dance or not interested in me? Had to be the former, right?

I felt eyes on me. The girls sitting at the far end of Edie's table were staring at me, their jaws dropped. In fact, so were most of the people sitting at the tables around where I stood.

Oh, man. I wanted to suddenly announce that it had been a joke, just a dare, ha ha. But Steve and Jared were suddenly at my side.

"What were her exact words, dude? Was she, like, totally blown away?" Jared asked.

"Uh, yeah, I think she was," I said. What else could explain Edie's answer? "In fact, she took off so fast that we didn't get the details down, so I've gotta go find her. Later, dudes."

I shouldered my way past them and headed out of the cafeteria, running Edie's strange response through my mind. *Sorry, but thanks.* Why?

Then it dawned on me. She obviously didn't

realize I was serious. That had to be the problem. She'd been so shocked by my request that she'd reacted without thinking.

Because no girl, in the history of Kennedy High, had ever before turned down an invitation from Nick Adriano.

Two

Edie

*She who answers in haste has more time to
ponder what might have been.*

—*Mama Ling*

AS I HURRIED down the hallway to my locker, I
was in shock. Total, complete shock. I absolutely couldn't believe that Nick Adriano had
asked me to go to the dance with him.

I mean, a guy like Nick Adriano absolutely
doesn't ask out girls like me. The shyest, quietest
girl in the school.

Not that I don't have friends. Although he
might have drawn that conclusion when he saw me
sitting alone during lunch. I was fairly certain that
he hadn't paid much attention to my social habits
before today. So he wouldn't know that usually I ate

15

lunch with Courtney Bloom and Sebastian Young.

But Courtney had an orthodontist appointment during lunch, and I had no idea why Sebastian hadn't met me in the cafeteria. Not that meat-loaf surprise was a big draw, but since none of us has cars . . . we don't have the luxury of experiencing off-campus lunch.

My heart was still pounding when I opened my locker to get my books for chemistry class. Why would Nick ask me to the dance? It made no sense. I wasn't in his crowd, I wasn't the cheerleader type, and it wasn't as if we were buds and he just happened to notice I was cute or something.

Which I wasn't. Well, not in the Mena Suvari, Tara Reid, Alyssa Milano way. I was sorta plain and wore glasses and boring clothes. Makeup and fashion just weren't big interests of mine.

Adam Spencer *was.* President of the chess club and the computer club. Just the thought of seeing him in my next class made my heart do this funny little thump. I'd been crushing on him for a little over a year now, even though I'd never actually spoken to him. I just admired him from afar. I sighed with frustration. I wished that I could get up the courage to talk to him, just once, just a few words.

Hey, Adam . . . loved the report you did on the dangers of radiation.

Ah, Edie . . . mine wasn't half as impressive as yours on nuclear fusion. I'd love to get together with you sometime after school and discuss your research methods.

Yeah, that was the great beginning to an intense

conversation that was never going to take place.

I closed my locker, turned, and shrieked. My heart was thundering so hard that they could have used it in the marching band. Nick stood there, leaning against someone else's locker in a way that hinted he had nothing better to do. Like getting to class was not on the top of his priority list.

He was so incredibly hot that I actually found it difficult to keep looking at him. I mean, he was movie-star hot. Dark features that hinted at a mysterious past. Brown eyes that he kept partially hidden behind lowered lashes so you were always wondering what he thought. He never revealed anything about himself.

So many rumors flew around the school about Nick that you never knew what was true and what wasn't. A different girl every night. Cutting classes. Detention at least three times a week.

A different girl every night. I had no doubt.

Nick Adriano might be every girl's dream at Kennedy High, but he'd never been mine. Yeah, he was amazing looking. He looked like he belonged on a motorcycle. But whatever it was that guys like Nick Adriano talked about, I was sure it wasn't anything that I talked about. I mean, what would we possibly have to say to each other? I doubted that Nick was into nuclear fusion. And I knew that I wasn't into cutting school and drinking beer and talking about cars or girls or whatever guys like Nick talked about.

What did guys like Nick talk about? *Did* they talk?

"It occurred to me," Nick suddenly murmured in a low voice as if he feared someone other than me might hear him, "that you probably didn't realize I was serious about us going to the dance together."

Huh? So he *had been* serious? Why? I normally wasn't slow on the uptake. My brain was having a total meltdown as he studied me with those brown eyes of his. I was having a hard time figuring out how to respond.

Besides, I was going to be late for class, and I'd never been late to class. It was sort of a pride thing with me. No absences, no tardies. Ever. But I couldn't seem to make my brain engage my mouth, and when I finally spoke, all that came out was a quiet, "Oh."

He stared at me for a second, those incredible eyes a bit confused. "So we're going to the dance," he said. "Right?"

My brain still refused to kick into gear. This whole experience was too weird. Like finding yourself cast in *The Blair Witch III*.

I wrinkled up my face in total confusion, but it didn't help me think any more clearly. "Uh, sorry, I can't," I managed to push out of my mouth before I rushed past him so I could get to chemistry class and Adam.

I practically flew into the classroom and took my seat. I glanced at my watch. Fifty-five seconds to spare. I cast a furtive glance at Adam, two seats down, one over. He was opening his notebook. He did it so precisely. Like a surgeon. Then he withdrew a pencil from his shirt pocket. He poised his pencil over the blank paper, anticipating the taking of notes. I understood that euphoria. Filtering the words of a teacher's lecture, capturing the key phrases on paper . . .

If only Adam Spencer would ask me to the dance!

"What's this I hear about you and Nick Adriano?"

I twisted around with a jerk. Courtney was sitting at the desk beside me. I'd been so absorbed in watching Adam that I hadn't heard her arrive.

I turned red. "What did you hear?"

My best friend—well, best *female* friend—stared at me like I was from Mars. "Edie! There's a rumor flying around school that Nick asked you to the dance. It was the first thing I heard the second I got back from my orthodontist appointment. So what are you gonna wear? We have to go shopping! I'm thinking pale pink with a net shawl and . . ."

I loved Courtney. Who else would (*a*) believe he'd really asked me and (*b*) assume I said yes and was planning my outfit?

I groaned. "Is there really a rumor going around school?" I asked like an idiot. Anything to do with Nick was news. Some girls who wanted to get his attention had designed a Web site devoted to him. Not that I'd ever typed in the URL that would take me to see it. But it was a well-established fact that it existed.

"So it's just a rumor?" Courtney asked. "Everyone's buzzing about it, so I figured it had to be true."

Everyone?

"It's not a rumor," I confessed. "He asked, and, um, I told him no."

Her eyes widened, and she clutched my arm as if she needed a hold on reality. "You told him no? No?" She shook her head. "Wait a minute. I had no idea you even knew him."

"Me either," I whispered. "It was so weird. Totally out of the blue. I couldn't figure it out. He asked me in the cafeteria, I said no, and then a few minutes ago he told me he thought I thought he wasn't serious. And he asked me again! So I told him no . . . again. I'm sure he wasn't really serious. It must be some sorta joke."

"Get over yourself, girl," Courtney said. "Your ego is *way* too big."

I smiled at her joke. "Why else would he ask?"

"Because he likes you!" Courtney replied.

I almost laughed out loud. "Yeah, right. And aliens really go to high school in Roswell."

"He *could* like you," Courtney insisted.

"Best friends are supposed to say that," I reminded her.

Just as the bell rang, Sebastian dropped into the chair beside me. He flinched. He hated being late to class too.

"Where were you during lunch?" I leaned over and whispered while Mr. Griffin began taking roll.

Sebastian's cheeks were bright red. "I was in the library, doing my chemistry homework."

I narrowed my eyes. I'd known Sebastian forever,

and I knew he was as diligent as I was when it came to getting his homework done. No way would he leave an assignment until the last minute.

"Did someone take your homework again?" I demanded. Sebastian was always getting picked on by guys at school, guys like Nick. Well, not Nick exactly, but guys in his crowd. Jerks who thought they were so cool that rules and regulations didn't apply to them.

Sebastian's face burned a brighter red as he nodded. "But don't worry about it. I remembered the answers, so it was no big deal to redo my homework."

"But you shouldn't have to redo your homework," I insisted. "Who took it?"

He shook his head.

"Come on, Sebastian, tell me who stole your homework. I mean, that's what we're talking about here—theft."

Firmly pressing his lips together, he averted his gaze and opened his chemistry book. I knew I'd never pry the name of the culprit from him now. I figured he had some pride.

Mr. Griffin started talking about molecules coming together to form different chemicals. I glanced over at Adam, who was taking notes.

Now, there was a true dream guy.

Adam was incredibly perfect. Unlike Nick, who only wore black T-shirts, Adam wore different-colored shirts each day. He had blond hair that kept falling over his brow, and he'd swipe it back like he was seriously irritated with it. I figured it interfered with his note-taking ability.

And he had the bluest eyes under his glasses. But what impressed me the most was that he always knew the correct answer, always raised his hand. Math, chemistry, English. He was a whiz at everything. A total genius.

I could imagine that a conversation with him would be so totally engrossing. He probably knew facts about things that I'd never dared contemplate. To have an evening sitting with Adam, talking about—well, just about anything—would be the ultimate.

It was funny. Ask any girl at Kennedy who would be her ultimate date, and she'd say Nick Adriano. I was the only one who'd say Adam Spencer. And Nick's the one who asked me out!

Something had to be up.

By the end of the day I was almost famous. I'd gone from invisible nerd to Edie of a thousand friends. Well, a thousand *schoolmates*. Suddenly everyone knew my name. I was the girl who turned down a date to the dance with Nick Adriano. People who never acknowledged my presence were now nodding to me in the hallways. I'd never gotten so many "hey, Edie's" in one day in my life.

With my backpack slung over my shoulder, I headed for the bus. Today was certainly one for the record books. I still had no idea why Nick wanted to go to the dance with me. All I knew was that I was more than a little suspicious.

Or was Courtney right? Was it possible that he noticed me and thought I was cute? Or that I was smart and nice?

Yeah, right. Nick Adriano didn't notice stuff like smart and nice.

Suddenly, out of the blue, Nick was walking beside me. I almost tripped over my feet.

"Hey, Edie," he said from that perfect, red mouth. "I'll give you a ride home."

I glanced at him, then down at my loafers. What was going on? Little alarm bells went off in my head. Normally I wasn't by nature a suspicious person, but his attention was too weird. There was absolutely no way the guy really liked me. No matter what Courtney might think. I wasn't stupid enough to believe that scenario, that he actually liked me, not for one single second—and I wasn't stupid enough for Nick in the first place.

He had a reputation for being attracted to girls who thought that brains were simply stuffed inside your skull so your head could keep its shape. Cute, hot, and dumb, that was his usual type.

Besides, he made me feel like the total geek I was. I mean, he never had a dark hair out of place. Had never worn braces but his teeth were perfectly straight. Didn't wear glasses. A zit had never dared appear on his face. He was never slumped over with the weight of a backpack on his shoulders. Did the guy ever engage in the activity of homework?

Add to that the fact that I didn't want anything to do with the type of guy who would pick on

Sebastian, and I had more than enough reasons to avoid Nick. And how did I explain all my well thought out conclusions to him?

Since my voice box seemed to be malfunctioning, I pointed at the bus and ran for it.

When I finally found an empty seat that I could sling myself into, I dared to gaze out the window. Nick stood there, hands on his hips, looking like he'd just encountered someone who'd escaped from an insane asylum.

Well, at least I wouldn't have to worry about him talking to me anymore.

Walking through the front door, I immediately smelled the aroma of sweet-and-sour sauce wafting out of the kitchen. My grandmother was cooking dinner along with her afternoon batch of cookies.

I pulled my notebook out of my backpack, which I dropped by the door, and headed into the kitchen. My grandmother turned away from the oven and gave me a big smile. "Edie!"

She hugged me like she hadn't seen me in years, when she'd seen me that morning before I left for school. Mama Ling was my dad's mom. Everyone in town called her Mama Ling. She had moved in with us five years ago when my grandpa died.

She missed him so much that for a while all she did was sit in a chair and stare out the window—or as she'd put it, she watched her memories.

"You talk in such cute phrases," I'd told her

back then. "I always think of fortune cookies when you speak."

And that's how Mama Ling's Fortune Cookies got started. She'd taken a course at the community college and learned calligraphy. Which I thought was totally awesome. I mean, my grandmother being a college student. It just proved a person was never too old to do anything she wanted to do.

Then she'd started writing her quaint little phrases on tiny slips of paper. She would bake cookies and slip the fortunes inside. She only supplied a couple of Chinese restaurants in town, but a lot of people collected her fortunes. Each one was unique.

I kept all her little sayings in a database on my computer. I was constantly amazed that she never repeated herself. She said coming up with her sayings kept her mind sharp.

"Did you have a good day at school?" she asked, her dark eyes bright with love. My granddad had met her when he was in the navy and stationed in the Pacific. She still had a slight accent that Sebastian and Courtney found absolutely charming. So did I.

There was something so amazingly warm about being loved and accepted for who you were. Here within my house I was Edie, daughter and granddaughter. Not Edie the geek.

"I had an interesting day," I assured her as I sat on a stool at the counter. "I had some time to myself during lunch to write fortunes since Courtney had an orthodontist appointment and Sebastian was in the library." I opened my notebook. "See which ones you like."

She climbed onto the stool and furrowed her brow. "So if Courtney and Sebastian are busy, you eat alone?"

"Yeah."

"But you have lots of friends," she insisted.

I really didn't want to get into a discussion of my social life or my stunningly nonexistent popularity. I shrugged. "I wanted to work on the fortunes. Some ideas came to me, and I had an incredible urge to write them down before I forgot them."

She grinned at that explanation. "Ah, that I understand completely. To give birth to a phrase is a joy."

I smiled. She always talked like she was writing out fortunes. Maybe that was the reason she was able to come up with so many. She'd had a lifetime to collect wise sayings.

I slid the notebook toward her. "So tell me what you think."

She peered through the half-moon glasses that sat perched on the bridge of her nose. My hands grew damp while I watched her read my words. It was kind of nerve-racking, wondering what she thought, wondering if she liked any of them.

It was a little like wondering what Adam might say if I ever got up the courage to talk to him. As a matter of fact, that was probably the reason that I didn't talk to him. I was afraid he'd find my conversation totally lame.

Probably as lame as Nick found it. He was no doubt still standing there, staring at where the bus had been and wondering what was wrong with Edie Dalton that she couldn't form a sentence that made any sense. Like I cared what he thought anyway.

I didn't, did I?

"Ah, very good," Mama Ling said after what seemed like an hour but was really only a couple of minutes. She touched my notebook paper. "I like this one. 'She who dreams can touch the stars.'"

I scrunched up my face. "You don't think it's dumb? I mean, you can't really touch the stars. I wanted it to be metaphorical and sorta deep, but not too deep."

"It is perfect," she assured me, squeezing my hand. "Just like you. I will use it."

"Cool!" I exclaimed. Using that word reminded me of my strange encounters with Kennedy's *Mr. Cool*. I furrowed my brow.

"Deep furrows mean deep troubles. What's wrong?" Mama Ling asked softly.

How did I explain this situation to my grandmother when I couldn't even explain it to myself? I twisted on the stool until I faced her. "There's this totally cool guy at school. Nick."

"Nick is a good name. What's he like?" she interrupted.

A question that I knew would be impossible to answer since she apparently didn't know what I meant by cool. How could I describe Nick?

"Well," I began, gnawing on my lip. "He's the

guy every girl dreams about. Really gorgeous, with these amazing dark eyes and dark hair, and he only wears black, and when he walks down the halls at school, everyone parts and watches him. He rules Kennedy High."

Mama Ling laughed lightly. "But what is he *like?*" she questioned, tapping her chest. "In here?"

I shrugged helplessly. "Oh, I haven't a clue. I haven't actually spoken to him except for today." That was a major exaggeration. I'm not sure stammering truly qualified as speaking.

"But you said he was cool," she reminded me.

So she had registered my earlier description of him.

"What makes him cool?" she demanded.

I was totally stumped. "The way he looks, for one thing," I said hesitantly. "The way he walks, like he owns the halls. Everyone knows him. That's cool."

"But those are things that you *see,* Edie," she chided softly. "Those are outside things. What is on the inside of this Nick?"

Mama Ling was one of those people who believed beauty is only skin deep and you had to look below the surface. She was always telling me that I was still waters that ran deep. I really didn't understand what that meant. Nick, on the other hand, wasn't still. He was constantly walking around everywhere, getting stopped every second by people saying hi, especially girls. Which seemed kind of shallow to me. "He's busy waters that run shallow?" I guessed.

Mama Ling laughed at that. "I do not think you know him so well. But still you like him?"

"Oh no," I assured her. "I mean, I don't *not* like him. Like you pointed out, I don't really know him all that well. And he doesn't know me *at all*. And that's what makes what happened today so totally weird. He asked me to go to the dance with him this Saturday night."

My grandmother's face lit up like a Japanese lantern, all soft and muted. "I will give you a manicure," she announced.

"Oh no, I'm not going. I told him no."

"Why?" she asked, looking not only completely baffled but disappointed as well.

I was actually sorry that I didn't have a date for the dance. But if I was going to go with anyone, I wanted to go with Adam. And the chances of him asking me were as slim as . . . well, until this afternoon I would have said that they were as slim as Nick asking. Still, I didn't hold out any hope that Adam would suddenly go insane as well. "I said no to Nick because I couldn't figure out why someone from the 'cool' club would ask *me* out."

She tsked and rolled her eyes as if the answer was as obvious as the nose on my face. "Because you are very pretty and very, very interesting."

I realized that I should have seen that explanation coming. She was my grandmother, for goodness' sake. She was going to see me as no one else did. Perfect in every way.

But me, I knew the truth. There was something

fishy behind a cool guy asking a nerd to the dance. That was simply the way our school was. There were the cool kids and the nerds. Yeah, there were variations in between, but basically there were the two groups. Nick and I were in different ones.

As I watched Mama Ling remove her latest batch of fortune cookies from the oven, I wished that I had more courage. I wished that I had just asked Nick *why*. *Why are you asking me to the dance?*

But there was no way that I could force that many words out of my mouth when I was talking to any guy other than Sebastian.

And maybe I didn't really want to know the truth. Didn't want to hear Nick Adriano, coolest of the cool, tell me that just as I had suspected, I was part of his be-kind-to-nerds personality-improvement project.

Three

Nick

Persistence is a tool of success.
—Mama Ling

"SO IT'S TRUE? Edie Dalton? You asked Edie Dalton to the dance?"

My ears were ringing as I looked up from my last slice of pepperoni pizza to see Angela, Lauren, and Megan, members of Kennedy High's cheerleading squad, wearing horrified expressions on their pretty faces. I was squeezed into a booth at the local pizza restaurant, Pizza Pie. Steve and Jared were sitting across from me, looking so incredibly smug. The moment of truth had officially arrived. Did I care what these beautiful girls thought?

I nodded, my mouth suddenly dry, the pizza I'd already eaten sitting on my stomach like a ten-pound barbell. I gave them a cocky grin. "Yeah."

"Why?" Megan asked. "Why Edie Dalton? I mean, she's so . . . so not in your league."

I couldn't admit to accepting a dare. That would sort of defeat my asking Edie to the dance in the first place. I leaned back slightly in the corner of the booth and rested my arm along its back, a totally uncaring pose. "She intrigues me."

That was actually true. My mind kept drifting to Edie and her strange reaction to my asking her to the dance. Why wasn't she interested? The million-dollar question. Unfortunately Regis wasn't standing before me, offering me a lifeline. I couldn't even poll the audience.

"She's such a brainiac," Lauren pointed out.

"Yeah," I admitted. *But that couldn't be the reason she said no,* I thought as if Lauren had tried to answer my question.

"So you two have absolutely nothing in common," Angela said.

Ouch! That hurt. I mean, I might not be enrolled in honors classes, but I'm no slouch in the smarts department. "We have a lot in common," I protested.

"Like what?" Lauren asked.

Good question. I racked my brain, trying to think of one thing. In desperation I latched onto something that meant nothing. "We both go to Kennedy."

The girls laughed in unison.

"So do I," Megan murmured. "You could have asked me."

I was beginning to wish I had. At least I knew she'd say yes. As a matter of fact, any of these girls would go with me if I just snapped my fingers. Only I couldn't snap my fingers because I'd told Jared and Steve that Edie had agreed to be my date. A totally dumb move on my part. If pride goeth before the fall, I was headed for a major splatter.

"We just don't get it," Angela mumbled as they walked away.

Neither did I. I simply couldn't figure out why Edie had responded as she had.

"The odd couple," Jared said once they were out of earshot. "That's what they're really thinking. You and Edie are going to be the oddest couple at the dance."

I couldn't argue with that. If I could convince her to go to the dance with me.

What was really starting to get to me, though, was the fact that Edie wouldn't only not go to the dance with me, she wouldn't even ride in a car with me! She'd declined my offer to give her a ride home this afternoon. She'd chosen a crowded, noisy, rattling old bus over my smoothly driving black Mustang inside which Macy Gray would have been booming. Made no sense whatsoever.

When Jared and Steve and I had arrived at Pizza Pie, I'd hit the men's room to check myself out in the mirror. Still the same. I'd even grimaced in the mirror—spotted no cafeteria leftovers wedged between my teeth. So what could possibly be turning Edie off?

"What a riot that she was so freaked out when you first asked her that she said no," Steve said, laughing. "Figures. What a geek."

"Yeah, good thing you tracked her down after school and let her know you were serious," Jared added. "She probably had to go home and lie down after."

I shifted on the bench as the guys cackled. Sometimes these guys were so immature. Then again, I wasn't exactly Mr. Maturity here either. After all, I hadn't even fessed up to the fact that Edie hadn't exactly said yes. That she'd actually said no *twice*.

I thought about finishing off that last slice of pizza, but I wasn't sure my stomach would welcome it. I wasn't exactly nervous, just tied up with concerns. I had to prove myself with this dare.

"Did you notice how dorky she looked today?" Jared inquired. "You know . . . when you were asking her to the dance? All those loose clothes. What's up with that?"

They both stuck their tongues out really far and mimicked those guys on the commercial who are always going, *Whassup?*

Man, how immature could they get? I knew they were just razzing me in an attempt to make me worry about my image. I did my typical Nick-nodding-like-he's-paying-attention routine, but the truth was that I was barely listening. I had a more pressing problem. How was I going to get Edie to say yes? To anything?

There was a reason the girl turned me down. And I was determined to find out what it was.

The next morning as I sauntered down the hallway with Jared and Steve, I was beginning to think that this dare was the stupidest one my buds had ever issued. I was no closer to figuring out how to get Edie to go to the dance with me. As a matter of fact, I was farther away from figuring it out. My original plan—ask her—had bombed. What should have been a walk in the park was turning into a climbing expedition to the top of Mount Everest.

"Hey, man, you gonna buy some geeky clothes to wear to the dance?" Steve asked. "So you and Edie can match?"

Steve had an irritating habit of picking up a conversation hours after you thought it had ended. It was like it took his mind a while to think of comebacks. But hey, he was my bud.

"Hey! Shrimp!" Jared suddenly yelled out of the blue.

I watched in stunned amazement as he shouldered past a couple of guys, grabbed a skinny dude's shirt, and started hauling him down the hallway.

"What's going on with Jared?" I asked.

"Oh, that's just that geek Jared's got working for him. Come on," Steve said, his eyes full of excitement.

He sounded like he was looking forward to something really fun happening. I couldn't imagine what, but I followed them into the janitor's closet

35

anyway. Steve closed the door behind us and locked it. *Locked it?* What was going on?

Jared hit the switch to turn on the light. Although calling the illumination that the bulb gave off "light" was really exaggerating. Shadows loomed around us. The closet reeked of ammonia and dirty mop water. I was wedged between Jared and Steve. And the guy Jared had hauled in here was straddled over the mop bucket.

I recognized him now. I'd seen him eating lunch with Edie a couple of times. Sebastian. He struck me as someone who would hang out with Edie. He pushed his thick-rimmed glasses up the bridge of his nose every time they slid down—which was about two seconds after he pushed them up. And he seemed to swallow a lot, like maybe his mouth was dry and he was searching for spit.

"Hand it over," Jared ordered.

Sebastian's gaze darted between Steve and me like he thought we knew what was going down. I just stood there nodding, probably giving him the impression that I did. After all, it would be so totally not cool to admit that I didn't have a clue as to the reason that we'd had to dodge into this cramped, smelly closet.

With a weary sigh Sebastian slung his backpack off his shoulder, reached inside, pulled out some papers, and held them out. Probably detailed secret codes or tips that would allow Jared to beat Starcraft or some other video game. Jared and I had been friends since the first days of Zelda, and even back then he was always bugging me to find out how he could reach the next level.

Personally, I never understood why he bothered to play the game when he was always looking for someone to reveal the mysteries. To me, the challenge was solving the game on my own. But I figured he was probably too anxious to see what the graphics at the next level looked like.

Jared snatched the papers from Sebastian's hand. "Thanks, shrimp."

Steve reached back, unlocked the door, and opened it just enough that they could both slip out. Which gave me a little more room to maneuver. This cloak-and-dagger stuff was really pretty amusing. Like Jared thought people would care about his lack of gaming skills. Then it hit me. That had to be it. He had a reputation for being tough. He probably didn't want to blow it by revealing that he couldn't master a video game.

Sebastian started to brush past me, but I put my hand on his shoulder. He sorta hunched his shoulders like he thought I was going to punch him or something. Suddenly I felt like a jerk. I mean, this guy was half my size. And even if he wasn't, why would I want to hit him?

"Sebastian, right?" I asked.

He just bobbed his head like he was afraid that he might be giving me the wrong answer.

"Relax, dude, I just want to ask you a question, okay?"

He straightened his shoulders, but he still looked

like he was expecting something bad to happen.

"Why won't Edie go to the dance with me?" I asked.

He looked as stunned as I had felt yesterday. His mouth dropped open, and his eyes got really big and round. I couldn't decide if he was shocked that I'd asked him a question at all or shocked that I'd asked him a question about a girl. Probably the latter.

Okay, so maybe the guy wasn't the brightest bunny in the burrow when it came to understanding girls. Even if the girl was his friend.

So much for that tactic. I wasn't making any progress with Edie at school. Maybe she felt like I owned this turf, and that put her off, made her wary or uncomfortable. I did kind of saunter around like I was ruler of my domain. I decided that I needed to approach her on neutral territory. "What's she doing today after school?"

He squinted as if he only trusted me as far as he could throw me, and judging by how thin his arms were, that wouldn't be far. "Why do you want to know?"

"Duh! I asked her to the dance, and she said no, so I wanna find out why." I didn't think there was a whole lot of risk in confessing this fact to Sebastian. It hadn't looked like he and Jared talked much even though they were sharing video-game secrets. I figured Jared liked dragging him into the closet so he wouldn't ruin his reputation by having people see him talking to a class-A nerd.

Sebastian started blinking the way Edie did, staring

at me as if he thought I was nuts. Maybe I was. Any other girl at this school would have shouted on the school intercom system that I'd asked her to the dance. Here Edie had obviously not even told someone she ate lunch with every day.

"So, dude," I prodded. "What's she doing after school?"

"Today we're doing our volunteer work for PAL at the animal shelter," he finally revealed cautiously.

I raised my brows. "PAL."

He gave me another what-an-idiot look. "Peer, Academics, Leadership."

"Right. I knew that." I really did. I just didn't pay much attention to the organization. After all, I had a life, and it didn't leave any room for club activities. "Thanks."

I opened the door and stepped out of the janitor's closet—right into the path of the girl of my nightmares. Edie.

I flashed her a grin and slung my arm around Sebastian's shoulders. Course, he did that hunched-shoulder-drawing-his-head-in turtle imitation, which only made him shorter, so I had to lean over. A totally uncool stance.

But I figured it was worth it to earn a few points with her. I mean, after all, I was chumming up with her friend.

She glared at me, her dark eyes smoldering. "Give it back," she demanded.

In surprise at her outburst, I slid my arm off Sebastian's shoulders and straightened. "What?"

"Give it back now!" she insisted in a low, threatening voice.

"Give what back?" I asked, totally stunned.

"He—He's not the one," Sebastian stammered.

Huh? The one. What was going on here?

Grabbing his arm, she hurried him down the hall as if I had contracted Ebola virus and they needed to escape before I breathed on them. I wasn't accustomed to people wanting to get away from me. I stood there absolutely still for the longest time, trying to understand what was happening.

What had she wanted me to give back? Something obviously belonging to Sebastian since he'd told her that I wasn't the one. The *one?*

Geeks. No wonder I didn't hang around them. They made no sense. Had their own secret code or something.

Shaking my head, I started sauntering down the hallway toward my first boring class of the day. I saw Jared opening the door to his locker.

The hairs on the back of my neck prickled as I thought about how intimidated Sebastian had looked in the janitor's closet. I strode up to Jared. "Hey, what did you take from the nerd?"

Jared slammed his locker door closed and grinned cockily. "His chemistry homework."

That made no sense to me. Why did Jared want the little guy to get a zero in chemistry? "Why?"

"Dude! My dad wants me to go to med school, so I gotta ace chemistry," he explained.

40

I nodded with understanding. "So you're comparing your answers against his?"

"No, man," Jared said in a voice that hinted my question was not cool and maybe I wasn't for asking. "I'm putting my name on his work and turning it in."

Not cool. I was on the verge of telling him that when it occurred to me that I'd sound just like my dad. Which would be as uncool as what Jared was doing.

Besides, it really wasn't my business, right?

Four

Edie

He who helps others might also help himself.
—*Mama Ling*

RESTING MY HEAD against the car's backseat, I had to admit that I was about to enter into my favorite part of the week: working at the animal shelter. Volunteering was a sign of leadership, so everyone in the PAL program had to put in two hours of service a week. When I'd seen the list of acceptable places to donate my time, I hadn't hesitated. I knew the shelter would be the one place away from home where I would feel absolutely comfortable. Animals don't sit in judgment on people.

Unlike certain "cool" people at Kennedy High who would remain unmentioned in my thoughts.

I'd been totally excited when Courtney and

Sebastian had decided that was where they wanted to do volunteer work as well. We'd been best friends forever, and it just seemed appropriate that we'd be working with animals that were known as man's best friends.

Sebastian always borrowed his mom's car on Tuesday so we could get to the shelter. Courtney sat in the front on the way, and I sat in the front when we were going home. Friends worked things out like that so everything was fair.

I liked sitting in the back first because it gave me a chance to unwind. I couldn't always hear the conversation going on in the front seat clearly, so I'd let my mind wander to pleasant thoughts of Adam.

He'd been able to recite the entire periodic table in chemistry today. I was so totally impressed. Not only because I could as well, but because I knew how difficult it was to memorize. I needed to excel in the sciences so I could pursue my interest in veterinary medicine. I wasn't sure what Adam wanted to major in when he went to college. I did know one thing, though. He wouldn't be a dropout. That role was reserved for Nick Adriano.

Sebastian had been tight-lipped about the reason he'd been in the janitor's closet with Nick. I figured it was just male pride kicking in again. Honestly, guys can get their priorities out of kilter sometimes. I was certain, however, that the closet experience had something to do with Sebastian's incredible disappearing homework. Maybe Nick was the go-between. Like a Mafia hit man or something.

Sebastian had said he wasn't *the* one responsible, but I couldn't help but feel that he was still somehow involved. I still couldn't believe that I'd gone postal in front of him. Had gone so far as to actually demand something of him.

The guy had looked totally shocked. No more shocked than I'd been. Before the anger had hit me, I'd thought he looked kinda cute standing there with his arm slung around Sebastian. Nick was way taller than Sebastian, and his shoulders were a lot broader, so they'd looked like a couple of mismatched bookends.

But then he'd flashed that smile of his, the one that looked like maybe he was hiding something. I couldn't quite figure it out. It was a gorgeous smile. I mean, everything about Nick was gorgeous. But the smile just didn't seem quite real.

Bang!

The loud, unexpected noise made both me and Courtney shriek.

"Hold on!" Sebastian yelled as he struggled to bring the shaking car under control. We bounced along until he maneuvered it off the road and brought it to a halt.

Breathing heavily, he jerked his head around. He looked terrified. "Is everyone all right?"

Courtney and I both nodded vigorously.

"What happened?" I asked, my mouth dryer than sand.

"I think we've got a flat," he responded.

"Oh, great," Courtney said as she dropped back her head. "In the middle of nowhere."

"It's not that bad, Courtney," I said. "He who looks for the bad things in life will only find the bad things."

She groaned. "Mama Ling would never come up with a fortune that lame."

I felt the heat burn my cheeks. I loved my grandmother's optimism. On her it seemed wise; on me it seemed naive.

Courtney twisted around in the seat. "I'm sorry. It's just that the shelter is on this country road, and no one is going to drive by to help us." She looked at Sebastian. "How far will we have to walk?"

"We're about five miles away. But I know how to change a flat," he assured her.

"You do?" I asked, trying not to sound too amazed. Sebastian wasn't exactly built for manual labor.

"Sure. Didn't they teach you in driver's ed?" he asked.

"They *showed* us in driver's ed," Courtney explained. "That's not the same thing as learning how to do it."

He pulled the keys out of the ignition. "It'll be a snap."

We clambered out of the car and trudged to the back. A rear tire was sadly deflated. Sebastian opened the trunk.

"There's the spare," Sebastian announced triumphantly.

"And the jack?" Courtney asked.

"Right here," he said, pointing to a black metal object.

"How does it work?" I asked.

He shrugged. "You just put it under the tire."

Ten minutes later we were standing there staring at the flat tire, glaring at the jack, and trying to remember exactly how it worked.

"Do I hear a car?" Courtney asked, suddenly spinning around.

Sure enough, a black car was heading toward us.

"Let's see if the driver will stop and help us," Courtney kinda whined.

"We don't know who it is," I reminded her. "You don't stop people on a country road."

But the car began to slow.

"M-Maybe we should get in the car," Sebastian stammered.

The car stopped.

"And lock the doors," Courtney suggested.

The driver of the car opened his door, and Nick Adriano hopped out.

Nick Adriano! What was he doing out here? Why was he suddenly everywhere I was lately? It was almost like he was following me or something.

Yeah, right. That would be the day.

Like him asking me to the dance.

What was going on here?

And why was my heart suddenly pounding and my hands growing sweaty?

"Hey, you guys got a problem?" he asked.

"Nothing we can't handle," I assured him.

"But we're not handling it," Courtney whispered to me.

"We don't need Mr. Cool's help," I whispered back.

Nick leaned against the hood of his car and folded his arms across his chest. He wasn't wearing his usual leather jacket, so his black T-shirt kinda stretched across his shoulders. Sebastian dropped to his knees and began tinkering with the jack.

Nick shoved himself away from the car and sauntered over. Sauntered. That's the only way to describe the slow, lazy walk he had . . . like he expected the world to wait for his arrival.

"You brains may know calculus," Nick said, "but it looks like you don't have a clue how to fix a flat. Move aside, Sebastian."

Sebastian skittered out of the way like a crab on the beach. I was more convinced than ever that Nick was the go-between. I wondered if he'd threatened Sebastian with those muscles of his that bunched and knotted up as he crouched beside the flat tire, set the jack into place, and began pumping it up. He really needed to buy his T-shirts in a larger size, I thought grumpily as I watched the seams strain to stay together. I angled my head. Or maybe not.

I'd never been one for gawking at guys, but I had to admit that Nick made me rethink the merits of that activity. I tried to imagine Adam coming to our rescue, kneeling down in his crisp blue shirt—today he'd worn blue, my favorite color for him because it brought out the blue in his eyes.

Maybe Adam would grow hot working and he'd remove his shirt to cool down. Beneath that would be a white T-shirt that his muscles would ripple against. Then he would turn his head slightly and give me one of his amazingly gorgeous grins and say—

"Edie, help me."

I snapped out of my daydream. It wasn't Adam looking up at me, but Nick.

"Help you?" I squeaked.

That killer smile of his grew. "Yeah. Help me."

I swallowed hard. "Like how?"

Nick held out his hand. "Hold these for me."

Not wanting him to see the sweat that popped onto my palm every time he spoke to me, I wiped my hand on my jeans. "Sure."

His fingers skimmed over my palm as he dropped the nuts into place. His fingertips were a little roughened, like he spent a lot of time outside. His hands looked really strong. I thought of those guys who cracked nuts open with their bare hands—which Nick probably did. Since we had absolutely zero classes together, I was fairly certain he didn't spend time cracking open books.

But he definitely knew the ins and outs of changing a tire.

In no time at all Courtney, Sebastian, and I were back in the car and on our way to the animal shelter. We thanked him and zoomed away so fast, you'd think we were headed to the announcement of winners of the science fair.

"I can't believe Nick actually stopped to help," Courtney mused.

Neither could I. Nor could I believe he was

following us. "Wonder what he's doing on this road?" I muttered.

"Probably checking out the latest, hottest make-out spot," Courtney announced.

Probably so. I wondered if Adam had a favorite make-out spot. If he would ever ask me to go there with him. If he did, would I go?

Sebastian pulled into the shelter's parking lot, and I had to put my romantic musings on hold. The animals needed my undivided attention.

I hopped out of the car just as Nick brought his black Mustang to a semiscreeching halt beside me. Out of the corner of my eye I watched Sebastian and Courtney hurry into the shelter. We were late, but I figured Sebastian's haste was due more to the guy getting out of the car than our tardiness.

Nick slammed his door closed and gave me a you-are-so-lucky-that-I-inhabit-your-world grin.

"Are you following us?" I demanded to know.

He rocked to a stop as if I'd just punched him.

I planted my hands on my hips. "Are you here to hassle Sebastian?"

"Hey, I just fixed his flat—"

"Yeah, after stealing his homework," I accused him.

He held out his hands like someone warding off a monster. "Hey, that was Jared, not me."

"You just went into the janitor's closet to look for some soap?" I demanded.

He shook his head. "I went in as a friend following a friend, but I had no idea that he was going to demand that Sebastian hand over his homework." He held his hands up this time, like a criminal caught with the goods. "Honestly. But now that I know what's going on . . . I think it's very uncool."

"And you want a medal for that?" I asked sort of meanly. I tromped up the steps to the shelter. What a jerk!

Five

Nick

To know someone, you must look below the surface.
—Mama Ling

OKAY, WHAT NOW? Standing in the parking lot, arms folded across my chest, I simply didn't get it. It wasn't cool for Jared to steal the nerd's homework, I had admitted it, so why was she being so attitudy to me? *Do I want a medal?*

Okay, I sort of got that I deserved her smart comment, maybe even the way she glared at me, but still . . .

What I didn't get, what I completely couldn't understand was why I had absolutely no effect on this girl. I glanced at my car. Getting in and driving off into the sunset was so totally appealing. Unfortunately my dad had taught me that you never retreat.

So with a heavy sigh I trudged up the stairs into the animal shelter. The reception area was empty, not that there was anything here that anyone would want to steal. Pictures of dogs dotted the walls, and there were some wanted posters, rewards being offered for lost pets.

I could hear dogs barking down a corridor to my right, so I sauntered toward it. It led to the outside, where a bunch of cages were lined up side by side. Not exactly cages. Very small fenced-in areas. Inside several were dogs. Every kind of dog imaginable.

And the mutts were making such a ruckus that the din was almost unbearable. Dogs of all sizes were jumping on the metal fence, barking for attention as if their lives depended on it. A few whined. Some even just lay in the corners, curled up into furry balls. They looked sad. I shook my head. I wasn't here to worry about some dogs.

I spotted Edie at the far end of the kennel, talking with a tall man, probably the director of the place. I sauntered toward them, trying to remain cool. I shoved my hands in the pockets of my jeans to stop them from reaching out to touch a black nose that was poking through an opening in the wire fence. That would be really uncool—to be seen getting down and playing with a mangy mutt. Still, it was really hard to ignore them.

I watched Edie slip a leash onto a German shepherd's collar and lead him out of the pen. All right! My brain kicked into strategy mode. "Hey!" I called out in a companionable sort of way.

The guy turned, and Edie stepped back, her big eyes blinking behind those glasses of hers.

"I'm John Logon," the man said. "Director of the shelter. What can we do for you?"

You can help me figure out why Edie is not into me, I thought. "I'm, uh, considering adopting a dog or maybe just volunteering."

Mr. Logon's face lit up like the lights on a Christmas tree. Edie didn't look so pleased. As a matter of fact, she looked downright suspicious.

"I was wondering if I could walk a few, test them out," I told him. I tilted my head toward Edie. "I was hoping she could show me the ropes."

"Excellent idea," Mr. Logon enthused. "Edie is one of our most experienced volunteers. Edie, why don't you show him where we walk the dogs and explain a few of the rules?"

"Sure," she replied flatly. "Come on. I'll show you how to *test them out*."

I fell into step beside her as she went through a gate that put us on a path that led to the road. "Was test them out the wrong thing to say?" I asked.

"Makes them sound like cars. Objects. They're animals."

Well, duh, I knew they were animals. We came to a halt as the dog made a pit stop. Then it started up again at a pretty fast clip. Edie didn't seem to mind. As a matter of fact, she really seemed to be enjoying it.

Her lips were curving slightly as if she might be daydreaming. I could see where walking a dog would be good for that. Something about the activity was totally relaxing. Maybe because the dog didn't yammer away. But then, neither did Edie.

She'd pulled her dark hair back into a ponytail that trailed between her shoulder blades. Usually she wore it loose, and I realized it kinda reminded me of the shiny coat on one of the black Labs I'd spotted back at the kennel. Her clothes today weren't as flashy or as loose. As a matter of fact, she almost looked downright . . . well, appealing as the mutt tugged her along.

I was hoping she'd talk, give me a hint as to the reason that she didn't want to go to the dance with me. But obviously fixing a flat didn't erase a trip into the janitor's closet with her best friend.

I figured that I needed to ease my way into talking about the dance since she still seemed more than perturbed at me. Besides, I wasn't exactly sure how to begin the conversation.

Girls had a tendency to talk to me nonstop, yammering away about anything and everything. As a matter of fact, I'd gotten pretty good at looking like I was paying a great deal of attention to everything they said when in fact it was all flying right over the top of my head.

The girls I had dated tended to talk about . . . well, things that I really couldn't have cared less about. Somebody else's breakup, a girl who had worn the same outfit to school on the same day as the girl I was with, what a hot guy Jason Behr was. Trust me, guys do not like to hear how hot another guy is even if he doesn't attend your high school and is paid to be hot on *Roswell*.

As callous as it might sound, sometimes I wanted to slip them some change and suggest they call someone who cared. I mean, I enjoyed having them around, but the nonstop patter could get to me.

I couldn't imagine Edie talking nonstop. I couldn't imagine her talking much at all. What I found strange was how much I wanted her to talk.

I was interested in what she did at the shelter. I'd always thought PAL was for the brainy kids who wanted to run for student-council president, but apparently a lot of it was about helping others.

She didn't say anything, didn't look at me, even. Just kept staring at the dog, which was sniffing around every tree and bush we passed.

We arrived back at the shelter sooner than I'd expected us to. I was still no closer to discovering *why* she wouldn't go to the dance with me or figuring out how to entice her into going.

She put the dog into the cage he'd come out of, slipped off the leash, and closed the door. "That's how it's done," she said finally. She started to walk away.

"Wait!" The dogs were barking and whining, and I could hardly think. "Maybe I could walk one while you're walking one. Just to make sure I do it right." Man, if that didn't make me sound like a loser. I mean, how hard could it be to walk a dog, but I'd blown my chance to talk with her while we were surrounded by the quiet. A person absolutely couldn't talk in this environment, where dogs were throwing themselves against the fence.

"Okay. I'll get another leash and find a couple of dogs that still need to be walked," she offered.

All right! I had expected her to turn me down flat. Like she had every other time I'd asked her to do something with me. Maybe she would relax a little more with me walking a dog as well. That would make us more equal. Before, we were kind of in student-instructor mode.

I crouched in front of the German shepherd. "Hey, buddy," I whispered. "I'm gonna get to the root of the problem this go-round. Yes, sir." The shepherd actually looked like he knew what I was saying. "You ever have girl troubles?" He was bobbing his head. "Yeah, I can imagine. But this is a new experience for me, and I gotta be straight with you, bud, I don't much like it."

"Here you go," Edie said.

I shot up and immediately adopted my nonchalant stance. It was embarrassing to be caught actually talking to a dog. Edie was extending a leash toward me. I followed the line from her hand down to . . . a little white fur ball that was bouncing and yipping. A total geek of a dog. I couldn't believe it.

I just kinda looked at her like she'd lost her mind somewhere between the German shepherd and getting the leash. "Isn't there a bigger dog to walk?" I asked.

"Nope. These are the last two. Sebastian and Courtney walked the others," she told me. The ball of fluff she intended to walk wasn't much of an improvement over the one she was offering me.

This dare was really losing its appeal as I took Yippy's leash and hoped no one I knew would spot me. Obviously Yippy didn't realize he was a runt because he tossed up his head and strutted outside.

I glanced over at Edie. She wasn't looking quite as relaxed as she had been before, so I figured that she probably wasn't totally comfortable around me yet. I needed to loosen her up a little bit if I wanted to figure out why she didn't want to go to the dance with me.

"Tell me that this isn't the kind of dog you see me with," I prodded gently.

"What kind of dog do you see yourself with?" she asked as we headed farther away from the shelter.

"Uh, you know . . . just some *big,* dumb mutt," I answered vaguely. I mean, I really wasn't in the market for a dog. It was just a ploy to spend time with her and figure her out.

She furrowed her brow and narrowed her eyes as if I'd insulted her. "Mutts aren't dumb."

I chuckled. She obviously thought I'd insulted *dogs.* "What? Did you give them an IQ test or something?"

"No, but researchers have. Not a standard IQ test, of course, because dogs can't read or write, but studies indicate that dogs that aren't bred for looks or for show—which a *mutt* obviously isn't—tend to be smarter."

I was taken aback by her response. "No kidding?"

"No kidding."

"How come?" I asked, wondering why it had to be an either-or situation.

"Well, people who are obsessed with the way things look don't necessarily care about how smart the creatures are," she explained with a pointed glare at me as if I fit into that category.

Okay, I hated to admit that her explanation kinda applied to me. I mean, my initial attraction to a girl usually happened two seconds after I saw her, way before she ever spoke and long before I discovered what kind of grades she made. As a matter of fact, studious wasn't even on my list of things that I liked about girls. Hair, eyes, lips, the way she wore her clothes . . . man, I suddenly felt kind of shallow.

"So," she continued, "when they're matching genes to get a beautiful dog, they might have to do a lot of inbreeding, and as a result they get some dumb dogs. But since a 'mutt' isn't a purebred, it hasn't lost its smart genes."

But I sure felt like I'd lost mine. "How do you know all this?"

She shrugged. "I read a lot."

"So Yippy here—"

"Yippy?" she interrupted, raising a brow in surprise. Her brown eyes sparkled, and her lips curled up in what could almost pass as a smile.

Still, I couldn't believe I'd revealed the temporary name I'd given this ball of fur. "A dog's gotta have a name," I informed her. "I can't just go around calling him 'dog.'"

"Her," Edie corrected me.

"What?" I looked down at the fluff ball, trying to catch a glimpse beneath its tail.

"The dog you're walking is a girl."

A total geek of a dog. If I had a dog, I'd want a Bruiser or a Spike. A manly dog. "Whatever," I said, trying not to let it show that I was bothered by this pip-squeak of an animal that had yet to shut its yap. "So the mutt here is smart?"

I could see Edie fighting not to smile fully, and I wondered why she wouldn't release that grin. Then she zinged me with it.

"She's leading you around, isn't she?"

That evening at home I was dipping fried-chicken strips into creamy gravy and fries into thick ketchup. My dad sat across from me, doing pretty much the same thing.

Tuesday was chicken night, but every night was takeout. As my dad would say, that was the advantage to being a bachelor. You could eat whatever you wanted, whenever you wanted. Which we pretty much did.

My dad and I were fairly tight, much tighter than Jared and his dad, but that was probably because Dad and I only had each other. I could tell him pretty much anything. He'd always been a great sounding board.

After all, he was a marine. And like all marines, he was really tough. He hadn't even seemed too upset when my mom ran off five years ago.

I mean, he got angry, no doubt about that. But

he didn't, like, cry or anything. He was the coolest guy, definitely.

It was important to him that I was tough too. Which was the reason that I never passed on a dare or deserted my buds in their times of need. I mean, marines did not—ever, for any reason—leave their dead or wounded comrades behind. That was the main reason I was slumming in the cafeteria this month. Steve was a bud in need.

Ironically, it was also the reason that I was in my current predicament. I mean, if we hadn't been in the cafeteria when the guys had issued their dare, they never would have spotted Edie. She was permanently cafeteria bound, and her shadow never would have crossed the door of Hamburger Haven at noon. But I'd been in the caf and so had she, and the rest, as they say, was history.

I couldn't believe how she'd zinged me this afternoon. Or how I'd felt about it. Actually impressed. As a rule, girls never insulted me, not even subtly. All I ever heard were compliments, as if I could do no wrong. As if I was perfect. I had begun to think I was. Edie obviously had no such delusions about me.

I lifted my fry out of the ketchup. It was looking pretty limp. I must have dunked it a hundred times while I pondered my current no-win situation. Convince a girl—who seemed not to realize that she was supposed to be grateful for my attention—to go to the dance with me. Or concede the dare. Convincing the girl was the only honorable way to go here.

But I needed some serious advice. I shifted in my chair. "Dad, you know how the guys and I are always daring each other to do things?"

He arched a dark brow. "Or *not* do things. Like last summer when you dared each other to not mow the yard."

I winced. I'd lost that dare hands down. My dad sorta had this thing about responsibility—which was inconsistent with the fact that he'd married a woman who wasn't responsible enough to stand by her man, as the old country-western song went. I tried not to resent the fact that my mom had decided to pursue her dreams away from us—I didn't even know what the dreams were—but sometimes it hurt if I thought about it too much.

And hurting was a definite sign that you weren't tough, which was the main reason that I had decided I would never let myself get into a position like my dad had. I was never going to "fall" for a babe. You know, head over heels, let her wrap me around her little finger kind of fall. Never. No way.

"Or last month when you dared each other *not* to fill up the gas tank until the last conceivable moment," he added.

My mouth twitched just a little at that one. We still couldn't decide if Jared running out of gas and having to walk six miles to a gas station meant that he'd won the dare or lost it.

I tossed the limp fry aside, picked up a crisp one, shoved it into my mouth, and talked around it. "Well, this is a do-something dare. The guys dared me to take a geek to the dance this Saturday."

My dad did something totally unexpected. He grinned with understanding. "My friends and I issued a dare like that back in the service. The one who brought the ugliest girl to a dance won and got the next night's partying paid for."

"Who won?" I asked.

Dad shook his head. "We never could decide."

"Well, for this particular dare, Steve and Jared selected the girl that I had to ask." I picked up another fry and studied its perfection.

"You're hesitant to ask her?" he prodded, trying to get to the root of my dilemma.

I tossed the fry aside, my appetite suddenly lost. After shoving my plate forward, I planted my elbows on the table and leaned toward him. "Uh, I didn't have any problem asking." I shook my head, still unable to believe what happened. "She said no."

Dad smiled again.

"I can't figure Edie out," I confessed. "She's not dating anyone, has no date to the dance, but still she won't go with me. *Me.* Makes no sense. Why would a nerdy, not-hot girl not want to go out with one of the coolest guys in school?"

"It took me years to figure out the answer to that question," he said in a fatherly tone that he seldom used. Usually we were just two buds carrying on a conversation. He patted my shoulder. "You're gonna have to figure it out on your own."

He picked up the cardboard box that had contained his dinner and headed into the kitchen.

Huh? That was it? That was his advice? Figure it out?

I'd been trying to do that ever since she said no. And I wasn't any closer to an answer.

Leaning against my black Mustang the next morning, I waited outside Edie's house. If Mohammed wouldn't go to the mountain, I'd bring the mountain to Mohammed.

I kept thinking about Dad's uncharacteristic Buddha answer. I didn't have years to figure out why Edie wouldn't go to the dance with me. I was down to days, hours, minutes.

I could always hope my appendix would burst so I'd have a good excuse to get out of this dare. But failing that, I had to persevere.

I straightened as the door to the Daltons' house opened. Edie rushed out like she still had that big German shepherd on a leash dragging her toward his favorite bush.

Halfway down the walk she staggered to a stop, her eyes doing that cute blink that I had figured out meant she didn't believe what she was seeing.

"I'm giving you a ride to school," I announced.

She got that belligerent look on her face, the one she'd used when she asked if I thought I deserved a medal. My stomach tightened. *Please don't give me a flat-out no.*

"Don't you ever *ask?*" she questioned.

All of a sudden it was as if a lightbulb went off in my mind. I gave myself a mental slap on the side of my head. I hadn't *asked* her to the dance. I'd told her we were going. So maybe she had a thing about etiquette.

"Is that the reason you won't go to the dance with me?" I inquired, trying not to sound like it was the lamest excuse I'd ever heard. Insulting a girl you were trying to impress was not cool. "Because I didn't *ask?* All right. I'm asking."

She pursed her lips together and glared at me so intently that I shifted my stance. Okay, so that wasn't the secret to getting her to go.

But there was a secret to getting her to go. It's just that it was locked deep inside her, and she didn't seem to be willing to give me the key. Any other babe would have not only slipped the key into the lock and turned it, but she would have swung the door open wide.

"Why do you want me to go to the dance with you?" she demanded.

She sounded seriously irritated. Didn't she realize an invitation from Nick Adriano was an honor any girl with a lick of sense would be thrilled to receive? And what was I supposed to say to her question? Admit that I wanted to take her because of a dare? Like *that* information was going to make the icy wall around her melt. So I did what any self-respecting dude under the pressure to win a dare would do. I lied.

"I think it would be cool to go out with a smart

girl for once." Funny how actually saying it didn't make it feel so much like a lie. I didn't mention that I thought she was pretty, which was, um, kind of true. I mean, I never would have noticed before, but now that I'd been hanging around her, I had noticed. She was pretty. Especially when she blushed the way she was blushing now.

Her cheeks turned a soft pink, and her dark eyes got all kind of . . . I don't know, warm looking. It reminded me of how I'd felt when Dad and I went skiing last winter and we'd sat in front of this big, roaring fire at the ski lodge. Cozy.

Finally her mouth blossomed into this smile that literally almost knocked me off my feet. Man, where had she been hiding that?

"Thanks," she said quietly.

I jerked my thumb over my shoulder. "So you want a ride to school?" I gave myself extra points for phrasing my request as a question. Before Edie, all I'd required were two words: *hop in*. And I'd have a babe sitting in the passenger seat of my car.

She kinda glanced around like maybe she was looking for the answer. Then she did this cute little shrug. "Okay."

Yes! Inwardly I gave myself a high five— something I didn't even do with my buds any-more because we'd decided that it was totally uncool to exhibit any type of emotional outburst. Low-key, uncaring, that was the epitome of cool, I reminded myself as I sauntered around to my side of the car while Edie slid into the passenger seat.

Once I was behind the wheel, I glanced over at her. She was concentrating on the windshield as if she was trying to figure out what creature had splattered there. "So will you go to the dance with me?" I asked, carefully phrasing the question in a way that I figured she couldn't find fault with.

"I still can't go," she replied.

My mouth actually dropped open. What did she want me to do? Drop down onto one knee?

Then she gave this incredible endearing smile. "Sorry, but given the fact that there are hundreds of girls who'd say yes, I don't feel that bad about it."

She laughed then, a sound that could only be described as merriment. I must have gotten that word from *The Canterbury Tales* because it sounded too old-fashioned.

I smiled at her as I started the car. But I still didn't get it. *Why* wouldn't she go with me? Obviously she realized that girls *did* want to go with me. She seemed to be warming up to me, so what was the deal?

"Which dog did you decide on?" she asked suddenly.

The more time I spent with her, the more I realized that she wasn't really that geeky. I mean, yeah, she was smart. She didn't stand out in a crowd. But there was something special about her, something that made you want to know her a little better.

Her eyes sparkled. "Yippy seemed to like you."

Yippy? "Um . . . yeah, I think she might have taken an interest in me, but I decided long ago to never let a girl wrap me around her little finger. Or in this case, paw. And as you pointed out, she was definitely leading me around."

Her lips curled up into this quirky little smile that was shy while at the same time triumphant. "There's a site on the Internet where you can take a pet-compatibility test," she offered.

"A what?" Was she serious?

"Compatibility test. Adopting a pet is a big responsibility that a lot of people don't take seriously. That's the reason we have homeless animals. People get a pet, thinking that they're acquiring a best friend, only what they're really getting is a child. Some people aren't meant to be parents."

Like my mom, I thought bitterly.

"So they get rid of the pets. But this site asks you questions and, based on your answers, it tells you what kind of pet is best suited to your expectations," she explained.

"No kidding. So what kind of pet do you have?" I asked, figuring she knew about the site because she'd taken the test—and probably aced it.

"We don't have any pets." I heard the disappointment in her voice.

"How come? You seemed to be a natural when it came to handling the dogs yesterday," I offered. She had been.

"My mom took the test," she said sullenly.

"And?" I prodded.

"Ants," she replied.

I laughed. "Ants?"

She nodded, that quirky smile of hers beginning again and growing. "The best pet for my mom is ants."

"Why would anyone want ants as a pet?" I demanded to know.

"Because they're cheap."

Shaking my head, I continued to chuckle. "What about you? What kind of pet is best for you?"

"Any kind." She turned her gaze toward the window as if she realized that she'd actually been talking to me and was somehow embarrassed by that fact.

I just didn't get Edie. She was so totally not what I'd expected. We drove the rest of the way to school in a silence that wasn't altogether uncomfortable.

But I was grateful for it because it gave me a chance to ponder what the secret was to getting her to go with me. I figured it was probably something as off the wall as she was.

I pulled into the school parking lot, turned off the car, and opened my door to get out. I didn't hear Edie open her door. I glanced over at her.

She just sat there, frozen in place, a dreamlike expression on her face. I followed her gaze to Adam Spencer, struggling up the walk with two backpacks slung over his shoulders. I guess he took every book in his locker home at night. The guy was a major geek.

I darted my gaze between Adam and Edie. Geek and geekette.

So that was it! She liked someone else. Someone more her own type.

Why did I feel so terribly disappointed? It was weird. I felt like I wasn't good enough to be liked by her or something. Did that make sense?

Six

Edie

Be wary of wishing, for the wish may come true.
                    —Mama Ling

"YOU LIKE THAT geek?" Nick asked me.

I glared at Nick as hard as I could, a sort of if-looks-could-maim kind of stare. Had I actually engaged in a semicasual conversation with this guy for a few minutes? What had I been thinking?

"Adam is not a geek," I informed him tersely. "Thanks for the ride."

I shoved open the door to his car, scrambled out, and started walking quickly toward my first class. How could I forget how people of his ilk—cool—viewed the rest of us noncools?

"Hey, wait up," he called after me.

Was he insane? Did he think he could possibly

say anything about Adam that I cared to hear?

Was *I* insane? What had I been thinking, to get into the car with him and risk exposing myself to a guy who thought the sun came up just so it could shine on him? To initiate a conversation—that floored me. Why couldn't I do that with Adam? It really wasn't that hard. Just start with a question that could lead into a topic that you knew something about.

I heard Nick's pounding footsteps and quickened my pace, but my legs were short, and his were so incredibly long.

"I can't believe Adam is your *crush*," he said as he fell into step beside me.

"That's not true," I lied, wondering how long it would take the gossip to spread if he told anyone. He would only have to tell one person. It was like from Nick's mouth to every ear in Kennedy High. "I simply admire Adam," I added, whispering harshly, hoping he'd back off or, failing that, get suspended until I graduated.

Adam was still struggling with his backpacks as we passed him. As usual, he didn't even notice me. Monday, I'd worn a brightly colored yellow-and-green outfit so I could stand out, and *nothing. Nada.*

I might as well have been dressed in boring black like Nick. Except that Nick's black wasn't exactly boring. *Intriguing* was more the word. It made him look dangerous. And amazingly hot.

Which brought my mind reeling back to a million-dollar question. What was Nick doing walking beside me? He'd brought me to school. He should have sauntered away in that lazy way of his; only it wasn't so lazy now as he tried to keep up with my brisk pace.

"Maybe you didn't notice, but nerd boy doesn't even seem to know you exist," he brought to my attention.

Oh, I noticed. I noticed every day. I marched on without deigning his remark worth commenting on. Tears stung the backs of my eyes. Nick had really hit the mark with his comment. I'd never gotten up the courage to even speak to Adam. Not a hi, a how are you, a what's happening. We had classes together. We obviously had things in common. Why couldn't my brain that knew so many facts find one thing of interest to say to Adam?

"Hey," Nick said softly, as if he'd actually noticed that I was upset, noticed something outside his cool world. "Despite what everyone may think, I *do* know how it feels to like someone who isn't interested in you."

Yeah, right! If he was crushing on Britney Spears, maybe. But even then I found his statement pretty difficult to believe as I rounded a corner. All the beautiful girls at Kennedy High spoke to Nick Adriano. Told him how wonderful he was. If they weren't using their voices, they were using their eyelashes. I often wondered if the constant, rapid batting of their lashes gave them a clear idea of what it was like to view the world from behind a strobe light.

"I'll make you a deal," he offered quietly. "I want you to go to the dance with me because I want to prove to myself that a brainiac girl would go out with me, that I can show a brain a good time. And if you say yes, I'll show you how to attract Adam to the point that Adam will definitely ask you out."

I stopped dead in my tracks and swung around to face him. *Dare I believe he possessed the power to grant my fondest wish?* I just didn't quite trust him. Not only his lame excuse for wanting me to go to the dance with him—after all, I was smart, but I wasn't the only girl at Kennedy who actually understood what a textbook was for—but also his willingness to help. And even if I did trust him, how could he possibly guarantee that Adam would not only notice me, but ask me out as well?

"How are you going to do that?" I demanded. I envisioned him hauling Adam into the janitor's closet and strong-arming him into submission.

He gave me a charming smile that weakened my knees. "That's my secret."

Looking almost innocent standing there, he actually appeared . . . hopeful.

Out of the corner of my eye I caught a glimpse of Adam, and my heart did its usual little flip—kinda like diving off the high board into deep waters. Against my better judgment, I was actually considering taking Nick up on his offer. But I couldn't. It seemed sorta like a betrayal to myself, a betrayal to Adam, and most of all, a betrayal to Nick.

I shook my head. "Nick, I can't. I mean, I'd feel like I was taking advantage of you." It just didn't seem right to go to a dance with a guy that you didn't like. A guy who was so not right for you. A guy who you were so not right for. Other than an ability to discuss dogs, we had nothing in common.

"Hey, you're not taking advantage. Just call me your fairy god-brother," he insisted.

I almost laughed at the thought of him waving a wand around. Almost. If he *could* get me a date with Adam, well, he'd be granting my deepest wish. But at what cost? Why did I have a feeling in the deepest recesses of my soul that I was going to regret this?

I sighed deeply. I never took chances. I never went where I'd never gone before. But here was an opportunity to do as my fortune had suggested—to reach out and touch a star. Metaphorically speaking, of course.

"Okay," I reluctantly agreed. "You've got a deal."

If Nick wanted to go to the dance with a nerdy brain, fine. Though I seriously doubted the guy could show me a good time.

On my way to lunch I spotted Sebastian heading into the library. Not again.

Quickening my pace, I caught up with him and grabbed his arm. He flinched like he'd expected me to be one of his tormentors.

Then he laughed self-consciously, pushing his glasses up the bridge of his nose. "Oh, Edie, it's you."

"Did Jared steal your homework again?" I asked.

"Yeah, but that's okay. Last night I scanned my homework, so now I just have to write it out so it doesn't look like it's a copy," he explained, a sad kind of smile on his face like he was hoping I would praise him for his quick thinking.

"Enough is enough, Sebastian. Since this creep keeps taking your chemistry homework and we have chemistry together, I want you to start giving me your homework first thing in the morning. I'll keep it safe until class."

"Ah, Edie, I don't want to trouble you," he said.

"It's no trouble, Sebastian," I assured him. "Besides, that's what friends are for."

"How about if I drop it by your house this evening? I don't want Jared to see me passing it off to you. He might try to take it from you," he told me.

And I had absolutely no desire to spend even a nanosecond in the janitor's closet with Jared. "Sure, bring it by anytime."

"Thanks, Edie, you're the best." He went into the library.

I sighed deeply. I didn't feel like the best. If I was the best, I'd confront the jerk taking his homework. But if I did that and still couldn't stop him from taking Sebastian's homework, he might figure out who Sebastian was giving it to.

Why couldn't life at Kennedy High be simple?

As simple as the tuna surprise adorning my tray in the cafeteria. Courtney was sitting beside me,

78

thumbing through her magazine. I was trying to come up with some more fortunes to share with Mama Ling, but all I could think about was Nick's incredible offer. What had I been thinking to accept?

I mean, really, what could the guy do to get Adam to notice me? Skywriting? Take out an ad in the *Kennedy Rag*?

Why would he even want to help me out? I still didn't quite trust his asking me to the dance.

"*Seventeen* has a test you can take to see if you're ready to make out," Courtney informed me as she turned a page in her current issue.

"Courtney, if you have to take a test to *know*, then you're definitely not ready," I informed her.

"I guess you'd make out with Adam if he asked," she mused.

"I might consider it if we were going steady," I admitted.

She lifted her gaze from the magazine and held mine. "Course, that's never gonna happen if you don't ever talk to him."

I pushed my tray forward, placed my elbows on the table, and leaned toward her slightly in a move that meant I was about to impart something of great significance. "Actually, it *might* happen."

My heart started thundering with the thought, the possibilities. Adam and I studying together. Adam and I sharing test scores. Adam and I walking the halls together, holding hands. Gazing into his incredible blue eyes. Him gazing into mine.

"What are you talking about?" she demanded.

Taking a deep breath, before I lost the courage to tell her, I blurted, "Nick offered to get me a date with Adam if I would go to the dance with him this Saturday."

Her eyes got big and round. "He what?"

I shrugged haplessly. "I know. I was stunned when he offered."

She narrowed her eyes in thought. "Why would he bother to offer?"

"He wants to take a smart girl to the dance and prove to himself that he can show her a good time." Even as I repeated his reasoning, I thought it sounded a little lame. Courtney apparently thought it sounded way lame.

"Why his sudden desire to date smart?" she asked. "The combined IQ of every girl he's ever dated doesn't equal yours. What gives?"

"Maybe he's just bored," I suggested.

"Bored with all the girls at this school fawning over him? I don't think so. There has to be more to it than that." She closed the magazine and gave me her undivided attention as if in the past two seconds I'd divined his true reasons.

"Maybe he likes me?" I offered lamely.

"You shot that idea down before." Courtney shook her head. "I don't know, Edie. It's a little weird. Whatever his reason, I'm not so sure your going with him is such a good idea."

She held up her hand in typical Courtney fashion, and I knew she was going to tick off the reasons.

She tapped her index finger. "Number one. Going to the dance with Nick might make Adam think you have a boyfriend."

"But after the dance Adam will never see me and Nick together again. Besides, Nick promised me that Adam would ask me out, so obviously his plan will ensure that Adam understands that Nick and I aren't an item," I explained. It seemed so convoluted, though, when I said it.

Courtney still looked unconvinced. She tapped her next finger. "Okay. Now for number two. What if you start to like Nick?"

I laughed. "No way am I going to start liking Nick Adriano. He's so . . . so domineering, and he has the manners of Jabba the Hutt." Okay, maybe he had stopped to help us out yesterday, but that was probably his feeble attempt to make amends with Sebastian. "Besides, he thinks he's Kennedy High's gift to girls."

"He is hot to look at," Courtney admitted.

"Only in a superficial kind of way," I assured her. "I could never go for someone who thought the cover was the only part of the book that mattered."

I nearly jumped out of my skin when Nick suddenly dropped onto the bench beside me, straddling it so I had to twist around to look at him.

"Hey, I need you to go to the computer store after school to help me buy a computer," he told me in typical Nick style as if I had no social calendar to speak of.

Okay, so maybe I didn't, but still I did have a life . . . and curiosity. "Why?"

"Because nerd boy works at Disk Us." With a satisfied grin he grabbed the cookie off my tray and sauntered away.

My heart was thundering. Nick was really going to do it. He was going to get Adam to notice me.

Seven

Nick

The heart knows nothing of strategy.
—Mama Ling

I WAS ON a mission. Introduce geek to geekette.

I was totally relieved that I'd managed to come up with a good "reason" as to why I wanted to take Edie to the dance. In a way, it wasn't exactly a lie. I'd never dated an extremely smart girl, and it was interesting to hang out with one. Sorta.

I mean, she knew lots of interesting facts. She didn't seem absorbed with gossip or trends.

We'd headed to the computer store right after school. As Edie climbed into my car, she'd looked for a minute like she was going to back out, but then she'd gotten this cute, determined look on her face and mumbled something that sounded like a

83

Chinese proverb. *He who doesn't try never succeeds.*

But as we were walking toward the store, I realized that Edie even trying might not be enough to succeed. She needed a crash course in attracting a guy, even a nerd.

"Okay, when we get into the store," I announced, "don't look at nerd boy like he hangs the moon. As a matter of fact, you shouldn't look at him at all."

She snapped her head around and stared at me. "Then how will Adam know I'm interested in him?"

"The object is to make nerd boy interested in you," I explained in a very teacherly fashion.

"Quit calling Adam nerd boy," she demanded, clearly irritated with the appropriate nickname I'd given the geek.

I hated to admit it, but the way she ordered me around sort of intrigued me. Girls were usually so grateful to have my attention focused on them that they never corrected me or told me what to do. They just followed, kinda like I'd followed that little mutt yesterday. Which was a disturbing realization.

I shoved open the door to the computer store and sauntered inside. Only my footsteps echoed over the tile. I glanced over my shoulder. Edie was standing outside, her hands planted on her narrow hips.

She wasn't wearing such baggy clothes today. As a matter of fact, she looked kinda cool in those jeans and that red top that left maybe a quarter inch of skin showing at her waist. She also looked slightly irritated.

I went back outside. "You know, I can't get nerd boy to notice you if you're not inside the store."

Fire practically shot out of her eyes. Probably because I found some satisfaction in reminding her Adam was a nerd. I couldn't believe she preferred the guy to me. Or more, that I cared.

Edie was just passing through my life—our time together would come to an end at the stroke of midnight Saturday. Maybe I'd give her an occasional acknowledgment in the halls. And maybe I'd feel some satisfaction when I saw her and Adam entangled in a lip lock in a corner somewhere. After all, without my assistance their lips would have never locked. For some strange reason, I didn't much like that provocative image cruising through my mind.

"You should hold the door open for me," she retorted.

I snapped my attention back to where it should be. On my present mission. "You're kidding me, right?"

Slowly she shook her head. Man, this babe wanted everything done for her. She was what Dad referred to as "high maintenance." The quicker I got her into the store, the shorter amount of time I'd have to spend in her company. "Okay, fine."

Gritting my teeth, I shoved open the door and stood there like I didn't have enough sense to walk through it.

"Doesn't your dad hold the door open for your mom?" she asked as she sashayed through.

That question dug into an old wound. "My mom ran off to California with some guy."

Her eyes suddenly reminded me of a Saint Bernard's, the dog that was always rescuing people. Sad and soulful. "Hey, I'm sorry."

I shrugged. "I got over it." And I had, but I'd made a do-or-die pact with myself that I'd never care too much about anyone or anything. It was the one way that I wanted to be different from my dad, who had cared . . . and gotten hurt.

We walked through the software and accessories departments. When we got to the actual computer-equipment department, I slung my arm around Edie's shoulders.

She immediately slipped out from beneath me and backed up a step. "What do you think you're doing?" she demanded.

Man, she was a total novice to the girl-gets-guy scene. "Nothing makes a guy notice a girl more than to see that another dude possesses her—especially when that dude is as cool as I am," I explained patiently.

Her face was like an open book. I could actually see her inner battle and knew the minute her dream to go out with nerd boy won. What I didn't understand was the reason there had been any battle at all. I mean, every girl at Kennedy *except* Edie would have fainted at a chance to have my arm around her. I didn't get Edie at all. I really didn't.

Still, I eased my arm around her narrow shoulders. She was incredibly delicate. Funny how she fit so perfectly against my side. Some faint, alluring fragrance teased my nostrils. I hadn't noticed yesterday with the odor of dogs around us, but she smelled really good. Exotic, almost.

Then a little green-eyed monster landed on my shoulder. Maybe I hadn't noticed it yesterday because she hadn't been wearing it. "Did you spray on some special perfume for Adam?"

"No, I always wear Jasmine. Is it too strong?" she asked, clearly worried that she'd engaged in a faux pas.

"No, it's fine. I just wanted to make sure that you hadn't done something totally uncharacteristic to get his attention. Because that would be uncool."

"And you think walking into a computer store with some guy's arm draped across me is characteristic for me?" she asked.

Man, I kept forgetting that Edie didn't blithely accept every word I spoke as if it were trimmed in wisdom. "There's a subtle difference between the two things," I informed her. "A guy understands completely. So just accept my judgment in this matter, okay? Stop questioning everything I'm doing and just play along."

She stiffened, and I figured I'd offended her. But then her eyes grew all warm and mushy looking and took on a dreamy, far-off glaze. I swore beneath my breath because I knew what I'd discover when I looked away from her, and sure enough, there was nerd boy. So much for her following my suggestion to look uninterested. She'd totally blown that opportunity.

And for a minute there I'd become distracted from my mission.

Against my side I could actually feel her heart pounding as she said, "Hello, Adam."

She sounded kind of breathless, which irritated me for some reason.

"Chemistry, right?" Adam asked.

Adam wasn't sure? I was so accustomed to everyone knowing who I was that it never occurred to me that some people weren't exactly known. I knew he hadn't seemed to notice her this morning, but I'd assumed he at least knew who she was.

Edie bobbed her head like an apple floating in water. Pathetic. Couldn't she see that this guy wasn't worth the trouble if he wasn't even sure which class he had with her? He probably kept his nose buried in a book and didn't know anything at all about showing a babe a good time.

"Can I be of assistance?" nerd boy asked, directing his concentration on me.

I almost barfed. *Yeah, you can assist me by paying a little more attention to the babe I've got my arm around,* I thought. *The one who's looking at you exactly the way that I told her not to, like you hang stars.* But nerd boy was apparently already calculating his commission on a sale.

"Yeah, sure," I responded. "I'm in the market for a computer. Something with a massive hard drive."

Nerd boy's eyes lit up at that. "So you want power?"

"Yeah, power, speed. I like my computers like I like my cars."

"I can relate," he said excitedly before he started explaining all the capabilities of the computer before us.

I wondered—a little unkindly, to be sure—if he would have been able to relate if I'd compared a computer to a babe. He was so totally focused on the demonstration and so not focused on Edie that my heart kinda went out to her. I glanced over at her to see how she was holding up under the reality that nerd boy was exactly that. A nerd.

But that fact seemed to be going right over her head. In stunned fascination she was hanging on to the geek's every word as if . . . as if he were me. Or at least me to every other girl but Edie.

She had never looked at me like that. What was going on here? How could she possibly be absorbed in this guy?

"So are you interested in this computer?" nerd boy asked.

I pulled Edie in a little closer against my side. "I'm not nearly as interested in it as I am in Edie."

Edie gasped, an expression of horror etched into her face. She pulled away from me. "I have to go," she whispered in a voice that sounded really tiny.

Unbelieving, I watched as she rushed out of the store. I could feel Adam studying me, so I turned back to him and shrugged. "She's pretty cute for a brain, huh?"

"Do you want the computer?" he asked.

Was he serious? I wanted to talk babes, and he wanted to talk computers? What could Edie possibly see in him?

"I'm gonna think about it." I winked at him conspiratorially. "But I'll let you know."

I sauntered out of the store. I was going to have to explain to Edie that she had to stay with me if she expected me to get her a date with this loser.

When I caught up with her, she was standing by my car, her head bent.

"Hey, Edie—"

She turned on me, tears in her eyes. Tears? Ah, man.

"You're supposed to make Adam notice me, not embarrass me!" she cried.

"Hey! I was making Adam notice you!"

"By saying you're interested in me when that's such an absolute lie?" she shouted, her hands planted on those narrow hips of hers.

But it wasn't a lie, hovered on the tip of my tongue. I forced the words back. I wasn't interested in her. In her quirky smiles, her fascinating conversations, her delicate shoulders, her dream to date a guy so totally not worthy of her. Was I?

Eight

Edie

Always expect the unexpected.
—*Mama Ling*

"I T WAS THE single most humiliating experience of my life!" I admitted, wondering how I was possibly going to show my face in chemistry class tomorrow. I could only hope that Adam wouldn't remember the way Nick had been hanging all over me or the lame lines he'd spoken in the store.

I was lounging on the couch in the family room, talking on the phone to Courtney. I'd come home, gone to my room, and cried over Nick's horrendous attempt to get Adam to notice me. How in the world did the guy manage to smooth-talk any girl at Kennedy into a date with him?

Right after supper, when I was a little calmer, I'd

called Courtney to bewail this latest fiasco in my short romantic experience.

"Matchmaking is obviously not one of Nick's strengths," I moaned.

"So you don't think Adam noticed you?" Courtney asked. I could envision her so clearly, stretched out on her stomach on her bed, her feet crossed in the air. I could hear the Backstreet Boys crooning in the background.

"Oh, I think he noticed me, all right, but not in the way that I wanted, with some guy's arm slung around me like I belonged to him," I muttered.

Mama Ling quietly sat beside me and pressed a finger to her lips to indicate that I wasn't to notice her. She was always doing things like that. Then she lifted a bowl of stuff that looked like guacamole. I nodded and closed my eyes. My grandmother was the coolest.

"He actually had his arm around you?" Courtney asked, clearly shocked, and I could see her scrambling to sit up. The background music suddenly fell into silence as if she didn't want to take a chance on missing any word that I spoke.

"That's right," I responded while Mama Ling began smoothing the goo over my face. She had all kinds of home remedies designed to help one relax and forget one's troubles. Herbal teas. Soaking your feet. She had one awesome shoulder massage that she always gave me the night before a major exam.

"Exactly how was his arm around you?" Courtney wanted to know.

"How many ways are there?" I asked. Mama Ling's fingers stilled near my cheek, and it suddenly occurred to me that she had offered to give me a facial because she was dying to know why I'd come to supper with red, swollen eyes that half a bottle of soothing eyedrops couldn't hide. Sneaky woman. But she was my grandmother, and I loved her.

"I mean, was his arm like hanging off your shoulders loosely, or did he have you pressed against his side?" Courtney prodded.

I grew warm as I remembered how wonderful it had felt to be tucked in against Nick's side. I'd never been that close to a guy before, had never expected it to be like the final two pieces of a puzzle being slipped into place. "We were standing pretty close together," I admitted.

"How close?" Courtney grilled. "Could light pass between your bodies?"

"Of course," I quickly answered. Although I really wasn't sure. I mean, our hips had been touching. Our chests. I'd needed to adjust my walk a little so I didn't stumble into him, which made me acutely aware of exactly how close we were.

I knew that he hadn't really wanted his arm to be there, that he was just doing it for the sake of keeping his end of the bargain, of getting Adam to notice me. But for an insane heartbeat I'd actually wished that his arm was there because he wanted to be close to me. Me, Edie the Nerd. That maybe he'd inexplicably realized I could just be Edie with no label.

"I hate to say that I told you so," Courtney began.

"I know, but you're going to say it anyway."

"What are friends for?" she teased.

Mama Ling placed a thin slice of cucumber on each of my eyes. It felt so soothing.

"I be back soon," she whispered.

I smiled. She had the coolest way of taking care of me.

"So what are you going to do?" Courtney asked.

"Call off the deal before it gets worse," I mumbled. "Since he at least tried, do you think I'm obligated to go to the dance with him?"

"Tough call," Courtney admitted. "I mean, he's willing to keep his end of the bargain, even if you don't want him to. So, yeah, unfortunately, I think you are obligated to go with him."

I groaned low.

"It might not be so bad," Courtney offered optimistically.

"Yeah, right. I think it's going to be a disaster." What would Adam think if he saw me at the dance with Nick? I'd figured going to the dance with Nick would be simply a matter of hanging around with him, but if he was slinging his arm around me at the computer store . . . but that had just been for show. He hadn't really meant it. He hadn't really wanted to put his arm around me. For some reason, that thought depressed me as much as making a fool of myself in front of Adam had.

"Edie, you've got company!" my mom called into the room from the door behind me.

I lifted my hand and wiggled my fingers, acknowledging that I'd heard her. "I have to go," I said to Courtney. "Sebastian is here to drop off his homework."

"He mentioned you were going to start holding on to his homework for him," Courtney remarked. "I wish we could get those creeps to leave him alone completely."

"Yeah, me too, but I can't see them listening to us," I told her. "We could talk to the dean of students, but if they found out, they'd probably pick on him worse."

"Yeah, and you know how Sebastian is. He has some pride," she added.

I heard Sebastian's footsteps. "Gotta go," I reiterated.

"Try to look on the bright side," she offered.

"There is no bright side, Courtney."

"Sure, there is. Things can't get any worse," she teased.

"I think that's what worries me the most. What if today's experience wasn't the worst thing that could happen?" I asked.

"Don't be such a pessimist," she chided. "Tell Sebastian I said hi."

"I will."

I lifted one cucumber from my eye and replaced the phone in its cradle.

"I've heard of turning green with envy . . . ," a familiar voice that didn't belong to Sebastian uttered.

The other cucumber fell into my lap as I bolted upright. Nick stood there, rocking back and forth on his heels, his hands shoved into the front pockets of his jeans, a huge grin spread across his face.

"Tell me you're not experimenting with some fashion statement you intend to make Saturday night," he commanded, his voice laced with teasing.

I pressed my hands to the goo on my cheeks. Could this day get any worse?

"What-What are you doing here?" I stammered.

"We need to talk. I tried calling, but I've been getting a busy signal, so I decided to come over."

"Without an invitation?" I asked.

"Hey, we're friends, right?" he responded. "I mean, how many people know you put gunk on your face?"

I wouldn't exactly call us friends, I thought. Conspirators in a plan that seemed doomed to failure came closer.

"It's not gunk," I muttered as I scrambled off the couch. "Excuse me for a minute, will you?"

"Sure. Looking at that stuff is giving me a craving for Mexican food." I could tell the guy was really fighting hard not to burst out laughing.

My cheeks had grown so hot that I was surprised the goo didn't melt off. I rushed into the bathroom and washed my face. When I looked in the mirror, I was grateful to see that Mama Ling's poultice had worked to eliminate my swollen, red eyes. I really didn't want Nick to know how much

I'd cried after I got home. It had been bad enough that I hadn't been able to stop the tears outside the computer store.

I just wished my mom had known that I resembled Jim Carrey in *The Mask* before she'd escorted Nick into the family room.

Nick was still standing when I returned to the room. I curled up on one end of the couch and waved my hand magnanimously over the remainder of it. "Have a seat."

He dropped onto the couch beside me—very close beside me. So close that I could smell whatever he'd patted on his face after he shaved.

He worked his shoulders more comfortably into the leather of the couch. "So was that Adam on the phone?"

I narrowed my eyes at him. "Yeah, right."

He shrugged. "Hey, I can always hope. I really don't think we did any irreversible damage today."

"We?" I scoffed. "The fiasco this afternoon was all your doing, bud. I made the mistake of going along for the ride."

"Give me a break, will you? Obviously brains have their priorities out of whack," he informed me.

My blood started to boil. "What do you mean by that?"

"I mean—" He stopped abruptly when my grandmother strolled into the room, carrying a tray.

Trust my grandma to be a little nosy. She set the tray on a small, round table between us and the television. "You are most welcome in our home."

97

About as welcome as a rabid dog, I thought unkindly.

Mama Ling tilted her head at me in a silent rebuke. I sighed. She wanted an introduction. "Mama Ling, this is Nick."

Nick's eyes about popped out of his head. "Mama Ling! My dad and I had Chinese takeout tonight. It came with two of your fortune cookies. My fortune was so right on."

Mama Ling smiled in that wise, gentle way she had about her. "What did it say?"

"'He who dwells on past mistakes will lose his chance for a future.'" He flopped back on the couch. "Totally accurate. I made a little miscalculation this afternoon, but I think I know how to remedy it. So I'm not dwelling on the past. I'm concentrating on the future. Anyway, what are you doing here?"

I tapped his temple. "Hello, in there! She's my grandmother."

"You're kidding! I had no idea." He leaned forward. "It amazes me how the fortune inside the cookie always applies so perfectly to me."

"It is fate," Mama Ling assured him.

"Can you read tea leaves or palms?" he asked.

I rolled my eyes. Was this guy serious? Seriously demented, maybe.

But my grandmother just calmly took his hand. She trailed her finger over his palm and looked like she was actually studying the lines embedded there. "You will soon approach a fork in the road. One path leads to happiness, the other to misery."

"Cool!" Nick said as he smiled and closed his palm as if he could hold her prophecy.

Poor guy. He was obviously too impressed to realize that life was nothing but forks in the road. Having grown up around Mama Ling, I understood completely how something could sound like it applied only to you, but it really applied to everyone. Just like fortune cookies and horoscopes.

My grandmother poured hot tea into two china cups. Hot tea? How many kids our age drank hot tea?

"Would you prefer a soda?" I asked, dredging up my manners.

"Nah, this is just fine," Nick answered.

Mama Ling moved the cookies closer to Nick. Then she discreetly left the room.

Nick turned to me. "I can't believe your grandmother is Mama Ling. Can she predict when you're going to fail a quiz?"

"With astounding accuracy," I assured him, "since I don't fail quizzes."

Nick leaned forward, snatched a cookie off the plate, and settled against the couch, his arm along the back of it, his fingers toying with the ends of my hair. I knew it meant nothing. It was just Nick's way of always touching girls. I'd seen him do this same thing a hundred times in the hallway.

Still, my heart pounded, and my mouth went dry.

"We need to talk strategy," he announced.

"Strategy?" I squeaked.

"Yeah." He slid his hand beneath my curtain of hair, his fingers skimming along the nape of my neck, making these delicious warm shivers travel along my spine. "You have really soft hair," he said as he lifted my hair and let it fall back to my shoulders.

"I rinse it with rainwater," I revealed in a raspy kind of voice that really didn't sound like me.

"Do you really?" He tucked my hair behind my ear. Then he touched my earlobe. "What do you wash your ears with?"

He was teasing me, and I wondered how I could be so stupid as to try to have a conversation with him. This was the reason that I never talked to Adam. I didn't know what guys wanted to talk about. "You wanted to talk strategy," I reminded him.

"Strategy," he repeated as if he couldn't remember what the word meant. "Right." Suddenly he stood and began pacing.

I pushed myself back into the corner of the couch, just in case he decided to sit again. I didn't need him unbalancing my equilibrium with absent-minded touches that meant absolutely nothing to him or lame conversation that made me doubt my intelligence.

"Obviously nerd boy was too busy working to notice you today," he speculated.

"Or maybe I'm just not noticeable," I pointed out.

Nick came to an abrupt halt. "You're noticeable."

"As noticeable as an unwanted zit," I remarked,

but something about the way he was staring at me—almost like his gaze was a caress—made me think maybe he meant something nicer.

He shook his head the way a dog shakes its body after coming in from the rain. "So what's something nerd boy does?"

I swallowed hard. Now came the moment of truth, the embarrassing moment of truth. I knew Adam's schedule like it was my own. Did I dare let Nick know that? I dared. "On Thursday, Adam stays in the library after school for an hour, studying."

Nick looked like he might be ill. Then he gave a brusque nod. "Okay. So tomorrow we'll go to the library."

I was on the verge of protesting, of pointing out that I didn't think that was such a wise idea.

But at that moment Sebastian walked into the room and staggered to a stop. His eyes grew really large when he saw Nick. He did a quick about-face. "I'll come back."

"Don't be ridiculous," I chided gently. "Just give me your homework."

I could see his little Adam's apple bob as he swallowed, like he thought Nick was going to bite him or something. Was that the way I looked around the cool people? Like I thought I didn't belong? Like I thought they were doing me a favor by letting me breathe the same air that they did?

I mean Nick was cool, no doubt about that, but he wasn't really that different. Okay, so maybe he was. He didn't let anyone intimidate him, and if he wanted something, he went after it. I had to admit his goals weren't real impressive. Like taking me to a dance. But he kept butting his head against the wall until the wall crumbled and he got what he was going after.

With great reluctance Sebastian handed me his chemistry homework. I tucked it into my notebook. Then I glanced up at Nick. He was watching me with this intense, speculative expression on his face.

"I gotta go," he announced. He snatched a cookie off the tray. "Don't forget our date tomorrow, and thank Mama Ling for the cookies." He grinned. "And the fortunes."

He sauntered out of the room, and I had this unexpected feeling of emptiness. As if we had unfinished business. As if something so much more needed to be said.

"Why are you dating Nick Adriano, of all people?" Sebastian asked heatedly.

"We're not dating; we're just friends," I assured him.

"Right. I've got eyes, Edie. I saw the way you were looking at him."

The way I was looking at Nick? What was he talking about? Because I looked at Nick like he was a possible friend? The way I looked at Sebastian.

Sebastian was making absolutely no sense. He blithely accepted some guy stealing his homework, but he went postal because of the way that I looked at Nick Adriano?

"Besides, I've also got ears. He told you not to forget about your date," he accused me.

I waved my hand dismissively in the air. "He wasn't referring to a date-date, girl-with-guy kinda thing. Nick and I are just getting together to study in the library tomorrow."

"I never thought I'd hear 'Nick' and 'study' in the same sentence together. I can't believe you're hanging around with him," he muttered.

"Oh, Sebastian." I almost didn't tell him about the whole Nick-Adam pact because honestly, some things a guy simply couldn't understand. This was one of them. Besides, based on Nick's success so far, I wasn't sure I wanted anyone else to know that I'd bought into his stupid scheme to get me a date with Adam. "I'm just helping him." Prove he can appeal to a brainiac. I didn't want to consider how much he was beginning to appeal to me. "And he's helping me get a date with Adam."

"Are you nuts!" he cried, so out of character for quiet Sebastian. "You're trusting him to help you?" He took a step closer. "Edie, I'm not buds with Nick, but I do know one thing. His kind never—and I mean *never*—do anything for anyone unless there's something in it for them."

"Nick is different," I assured him, even though I'd thought the same thing myself over and over.

"Get real, Edie. If you hang out with Nick, you're asking for trouble," he insisted.

I shifted uneasily on the couch. "I really don't think so, Sebastian."

He shook his head as if he couldn't believe what he was hearing. "I need to get home and finish up my homework."

Sebastian practically stomped out of the room.

Great. Now one of my best friends was mad at me.

Nine

Edie

*The challenge of a mystery lies not in its solution
but in the journey you take to uncover it.*

—*Mama Ling*

"NOW, REMEMBER," NICK reminded me as we walked toward the library, "don't give Adam that you-hang-the-stars look."

"I don't look at Adam like that," I chided.

Nick came to an abrupt halt, put his hands on my shoulders, and turned me so I faced him squarely. "Edie, when you look at the guy, 'crushing on you' flashes in your eyes like a neon sign."

"It does not," I mumbled petulantly.

"Look at me," he ordered.

I narrowed my eyes and glared at him.

"You look seriously aggravated with me," he muttered.

"I *am* seriously aggravated with you," I blurted.

"Good. Now back it up to 'I don't care about you,'" he instructed me as if he were the director in a school play.

How could I keep forgetting that all this—his interest in me, his willingness to help—was all a game designed to find out if he could show a brain a good time? No matter how much he was doing for me, when it came right down to it, the center of the deal was Nick. Nick was always the focal point of everything.

Just as Sebastian had warned me. I'd gone into this deal from the beginning knowing what Nick was like. I couldn't get irritated at him now for meeting all my expectations. I took a deep breath and let some of the anger drain away.

"That's better," Nick praised me as he draped his arm across my shoulders.

"Do you have to do that?" I asked.

"Trust me, Edie, if he thinks I can't keep my hands off you, he's going to wonder what he's missing. He'll ask you out." He nudged me in closer to his side.

"Just like yesterday, right?" I admonished, trying to distract myself from noticing how nice it felt to be wedged up against him.

"Let's forget yesterday," he suggested. "Remember my fortune. I think it could easily apply to you."

"Of course it could," I told him. "All fortunes apply to everyone."

"No, they don't," he insisted.

"Nick." I wiggled out from his embrace, put my hands on his shoulders, and turned him to face me. "Look at me."

He did. In that lazy way of his that was so incredibly intense. His eyes seemed to darken, the pupils dilating. His lids were half lowered as if he was on the verge of dreaming about me. He really had extraordinary eyes that somehow made it feel like he was touching your heart and soul with just a glance.

Only this was more than a glance. This was a gaze hot enough to shatter a cold heart. And mine was anything but cold. His eyes held mine with such fervor that my knees started to weaken and I forgot how to breathe.

"Fortunes?" he rasped in a thick voice as if he too had felt the magnetic attraction shimmering between us.

Shaking my head, I broke the connection. "Uh, fortunes." I breathed deeply. "They're designed so everyone can see themselves in them, based on their perspective. It's a real art to create a good fortune."

"Whatever," he said briskly as he slung his arm around me. "Let's get this Adam encounter under way."

My nerves were so close to the surface that I felt like little pinpricks were traveling over my skin as Nick opened the door for me without me having to remind him. Maybe he could be trained after all. Just like a young puppy.

Whoa. I had no desire to train Nick. Besides, I was losing sight of my goal—it wasn't attracting Nick. It was attracting Adam. Getting Adam to notice me and ask me out. The realization of a long-held dream.

Forcing myself to concentrate on the task at hand, I immediately spotted Adam sitting at his customary table, his head bent over a book, a pencil poised over his notebook paper. My heart did its little flip. But it didn't leap as high or dive as deeply. Which made no sense. Adam was still my crush.

Nick made a beeline for Adam's table. I planted my feet so he couldn't drag me with him. His arm slipped off me as he halted. I really could think a lot more clearly when his scent wasn't wafting around me and his arm wasn't holding me as if I were his.

"This way." I started to lead him toward the corner table where I usually sat and drooled over Adam.

"No way," Nick whispered, his breath ruffling my hair as he leaned close, obviously aware of library rules about silence. "He can't notice you all the way over there."

So without even asking—in typical Nick fashion—he seated us at Adam's table.

Adam looked up, his brow furrowed like he was seriously annoyed. I felt my face turn five different shades of red. The fact that Nick was leaning back in his chair with his hand resting on *my* chair so his fingers could toy with the ends of my hair didn't help my embarrassment fade.

Relax, I ordered myself. I was on familiar terrain, had logged hours in the library. I cleared my throat. "Are you researching your history paper, Adam?" It sounded so neat to say his name to his face.

"Yes," he answered succinctly.

"So are we," I assured him. I quietly placed my notebook and a book on the table.

Adam returned to whatever heavy thought processes he'd been engaged in before our arrival. Nick was so totally right. Sitting here was better. I could watch the way Adam wrote—so precisely. And he was so totally focused. I imagined how neat it would feel to have that attention focused so intently on me.

Nick still had his arm around my shoulders, even though we were sitting side by side. I could feel his gaze on me. So intense. Sorta like what I wanted from Adam. Like it had been in the hallway. Still, I knew it wasn't real, just like having his arm around me was false. He was only doing it as part of the bargain. A ploy. Misleading. A way to get Adam to notice me.

And I really wished Adam would notice me so Nick could stop the charade. Adam was the one I was interested in. Adam was the one I wanted. But I couldn't stop wondering if Nick saw anything in me except a nerd. Did he even possess the ability to look beyond the outer shell of a person to see the inner vulnerabilities?

He leaned close until I could feel his breath skimming along my cheek. A shiver shuddered down my spine. I tried to remain focused on Adam, but I was so totally aware of Nick. And how hot he was.

"You have really exotic eyes," he said in a low voice.

My eyes were a lot like my grandmother's, slightly Asian. Adam glanced up and glared at Nick. *Look at me,* I thought, *pay attention to me, not Nick. Nick gets attention all the time. He's used to it. I'm not.*

"You ever notice Edie's eyes?" Nick asked, like there was something truly special about them.

Adam heaved a heavy sigh, which unfortunately I could relate to and completely understood. There was nothing worse than having your concentration interrupted. Again and again and again.

I opened my mouth to apologize, but as if he knew exactly what I was going to do, Nick placed his finger against my lips, causing them to tingle.

"You've got such an incredible kissable mouth," he whispered. "I think about kissing you a lot. . . ."

He let the thought linger, unspoken, and my imagination went wild. My breath backed up in my lungs. He almost sounded like he truly meant it. That he actually did think of kissing me. I'd never really noticed Nick's lips, but they looked kissable as well. Although unlike mine, I had a feeling his had lots of experience.

Adam slammed his book closed, gathered up his stuff, and walked away.

Mortification rammed into me.

"What is that guy's problem?" Nick asked as if he were completely dumbfounded.

"Maybe we were disturbing him," I suggested, grateful that my voice sounded almost normal.

Nick jerked his head back as if I'd offended him. "I was just trying to get the guy to notice you."

"Silence would have worked better," I assured him.

He shrugged as if he was suddenly bored. "Whatever. Let's go."

I opened my history book. "You can leave. I have a research paper to work on and an hour before my mom gets here to pick me up."

"Hey, I can take you home," he offered.

I simply shook my head. I'd really had enough of Nick in the last twenty-four hours. "No thanks."

Ten

Nick

The journey to friendship begins with a step.
—*Mama Ling*

MAN, SITTING HERE in the library, watching
Edie with her nose buried in a dusty book,
Adam nowhere to be seen, all I could think was
that nerds had their priorities all mixed up. I mean,
if given the choice between reading about some
dead guy or talking about a warm, flesh-and-blood
girl, I was going to choose the girl every time.

What made this situation worse was that Edie
appeared to be seriously aggravated with me. And I
couldn't figure out why.

So I had paid her a couple of compliments. She
did have nice lips—real nice. They kinda looked
moist, but not wet, so I knew she wore something

on them because she didn't have a habit of licking them. And she had gorgeous eyes, really exotic looking. They were oval and slanted up.

My attention was drawn back to her mouth. . . . I couldn't stop wondering what it would be like to press my lips against it. The word *hot* exploded in my mind. It would definitely be hot, with her sassy little comebacks.

Most girls who let me kiss them just stood there and accepted what I offered, my mouth doing all the work. But with Edie . . . I just couldn't see that happening. I wouldn't be kissing her. We'd be kissing each other. . . . I liked things slow . . . and we'd probably start out that way, and then she'd get impatient and pick up the tempo, and when my heart started pumping so hard that I could hear it thundering between my ears, I'd have to slow us down. She would moan in protest, but she'd give in anyway . . . for a while.

Man, I jerked myself out of that fantasy. Beads of sweat had popped out on my brow, and my heart was racing. Kissing for me was usually automatic. It wasn't something I pondered beyond wondering when it was the right time to make my move.

But here I was—sitting, imagining kissing her, and seeing it in some sort of slow motion. I needed a major distraction. No way was I kissing a nerd in the boring library.

I snatched the pencil out of her hand and scribbled on her notebook paper, *Let's go have some fun.*

She slid her gaze toward me. "I am having fun."

114

"Impossible," I said, but my voice sounded kinda hoarse. No doubt the last vestiges of thinking about that kiss. "You're doing boring research."

"The first serial murder in Texas is hardly boring," she replied absently as she turned her attention back to the magazine she was reading.

"You're kidding, right?"

She finally lifted her gaze from the article and looked at me head-on, obviously not delighted that I was questioning her. Man, a guy could totally get lost in the brown depths of those eyes. "I meant to ask, who did it?"

"They're not sure. The murders took place in Austin. Some people speculate that Jack the Ripper was responsible," she informed me.

I wasn't a total dunce. I'd seen the movie. "Jack the Ripper killed women in London."

"But during this time period, shortly after he had killed the London women, no other women were killed with his MO. So some think he might have gone to Austin and done the dirty deed." Her eyes were flashing with excitement at the prospect of proving this theory.

"Like he was on vacation and couldn't resist knocking off a few women?" I asked.

She shrugged. "Maybe." She reached for her notebook. "These are some articles I copied from the archives at the city library. Do you want to read them, see if you can find any connection I might have missed?"

"Sure. Why not?" And before I knew it, we

were researching articles and reading about a series of related murders in Texas in the late 1800s.

Fascinating. A bloodied footprint had been left at one crime scene. They'd actually had a suspect step on it to see if his foot was the right size.

I felt a nudge on my shoulder and looked up from an account of one of the murder victims who was supposedly cheating on her husband. Now he was a suspect. But since Jack the Ripper tended to kill women with loose morals, maybe he'd done the woman in.

Edie had this cute little smile on her face. "I have to go." She tapped her watch. "My mom will be waiting."

An hour had already passed? Standing, I folded the paper she had given me to make notes on and slipped it in my back hip pocket. Carrying a backpack was so not cool.

I followed her through the library and opened the door for her. That was kind of scary. It was getting to be automatic. I shuddered at the thought.

"I promise I'll talk with Adam," I told her as we headed outside.

She shook her head. "Please don't."

Sitting in history class the next day, I only half listened as Mr. Tanner lectured. The class was dull. All my classes were dull, totally nonchallenging.

Unlike Edie, I wasn't in any honors class. In my history class we weren't given a research-paper assignment—like maybe Mr. Tanner thought it was above our abilities.

Until this moment it had never dawned on me why I disliked school so much and thought it was a total waste of time. Now I was starting to figure it out. It was utterly boring.

I had actually enjoyed helping Edie research her paper the day before, and I thought I would enjoy writing the paper even more, putting the facts together and trying to figure out who really had committed those murders.

But I had never applied myself to studies because I'd always thought brainy kids were uncool. But Edie knew about so many interesting things. So why couldn't I interest Adam in her? I had never expected it to be this hard.

Suddenly it hit me. I had never tried to interest a guy in a girl before. I mean, I had always wanted all the girls. I had never wanted to see one taken from me. I was obviously using the wrong approach. I needed to rethink my strategy.

I glanced over at Jared. This *was* history class, but he had his chemistry book open and was scribbling away like crazy.

I never could figure out how he had managed to get into honors chemistry. I guessed his dad pulled a few strings with the counselor or something. I leaned toward him. "What are you doing?" I kept my voice low so Mr. Tanner wouldn't call on me to answer some question like why the Union built Arlington Cemetery on Robert E. Lee's property.

"That nerd Sebastian stopped doing his

homework," he whispered harshly. He was seriously aggravated.

I straightened. My admiration for Edie grew. Sebastian hadn't stopped doing his homework. He had found a safer notebook to keep it in.

I considered telling Jared the truth—after all, he was my friend—but if his stealing homework wasn't my business three days ago, it wasn't my business now.

I turned my attention back to the problem at hand, trying to figure out how to make Adam notice Edie. She had a sense of humor. I'd discovered that when we were walking the dogs. She was loyal to friends. Look how she was sticking up for Sebastian. She had a killer smile.

I needed to put her in some situation with Adam where he could see that smile. If that gorgeous mouth of hers didn't reel him in then, there was no hope for the guy.

Of course, finding that kind of a situation was easier said than done. But maybe it was only difficult because I wasn't looking hard enough. Did I really want to see nerd boy date her?

She deserved someone better. Someone cool. And I didn't mean that the way it sounded. I meant that nerd boy seemed like jerk boy.

I knew that Edie thought I was some sort of a jerk, but nerd boy was the real one.

Otherwise he'd be tripping over his feet to get her to notice *him*.

Eleven

Edie

Even a butterfly must change before it can be beautiful.
—*Mama Ling*

FRIDAY EVENING COURTNEY and I were cruising the mall. I had no idea what to wear to the dance tomorrow night.

It was my first dance. Actually it was my first date, but if I thought about that, I began to get really anxious. Although it wasn't the prom, I didn't want Nick to be totally embarrassed to be seen with me. I wished more than ever that I hadn't agreed to go with him.

This deal had really turned out to be a disaster. I mean, getting dates for girls with other guys was obviously not Nick's forte.

Besides, if I was truly honest with myself—which

I always tried to be—I sorta found myself wishing that Nick had asked me because he thought I was cute or something, not because he wanted to know what it was like to date a smart girl.

There's nothing wrong with a guy admiring a girl's intelligence, but I didn't have the impression that Nick admired anything about me. My smarts were simply a challenge to him. *I'll take a smart girl out.* Kinda like saying, "I'll take a blonde or brunette, a short girl, a heavy girl."

Nick seemed to be into using labels. I was a brainiac. Adam was a nerd. Nick was cool.

The only reason I could see for a guy to really take a girl out was because he *liked* her.

I knew that I'd never look like the cute girls in school and I'd never be *cool.* I knew that I was more interested in history than makeup, more interested in helping others than combing the mall, looking for the perfect outfit.

"You know what you need? Contacts," Courtney announced.

Her outburst jarred me out of my thoughts.

"No way am I sticking something in my eye," I told her.

I finally noticed our surroundings. We were standing in front of one of those glasses-in-an-hour places.

"Contacts aren't that bad," she assured me. "I'll get some if you do."

I had looked at the world through frames for as long as I could remember. But I could tell that

Courtney really wanted the contacts. It was just that it was one of those things that was a little bit frightening. Like getting your ears pierced. The sound of that piercing gun was enough to make you jump.

I remembered how big Courtney's eyes had gotten when she was waiting to get her ears pierced—waiting to get hers done because I wanted to get mine done . . . but not alone.

And how awful our hair had looked the time that we decided to cut each other's hair so we could use the money our moms gave us for a haircut on a Backstreet Boys CD instead.

Now all she wanted me to do was stick something in my eye. Sure, no problem, Courtney. After all, what are friends for?

I wouldn't have to actually use them.

I slipped my arm through hers. "What the heck. Let's do it."

"I like this Nick," Mama Ling proclaimed softly.

I almost let my eyes fly open—which would have been a total disaster since Mama Ling was applying eye shadow to the lids. She'd offered to help me get ready. "Even a flower must unfurl its petals to be appreciated," she'd said.

Well, I felt like this flower's petals were close to wilting as my stomach tightened with each passing hour. I couldn't believe that I was actually going to the dance with Nick Adriano. Of course everyone at school knew. Nick can't sneeze without everyone knowing.

I'd never thought about the pressure that might be on him—being so popular and all. I mean if I was out sick, no one noticed. But Nick was constantly watched.

I had been as well this week. Girls had given me the once-over in the hallways as if they were trying to figure out what I possessed that they didn't. What was it about me that appealed to Nick?

I'd been so tempted so many times to yell, "My brains! My brains are the only thing about me that would remotely come close to attracting a guy like Nick."

I was really proud of the fact that I was smart, had good grades, was admired by the teachers . . . but I wasn't sure that I really wanted to be known for my brains.

But wasn't that the reason that I liked Adam? Other than the fact that he knew every answer to every question and practically lived with his face buried in a book, what did I know about him? Other than the fact that he never noticed me—even when I was with Nick, Adam seemed to look right past me.

"Don't furrow your brow," Mama Ling admonished.

I forced myself to relax. Why was it taking so long to unfurl my petals? I figured because I had so few to work with.

"Tell me more about this Nick," Mama Ling prodded.

I shrugged slightly. "We're just, you know . . . friends."

"But you like him?"

"Well . . . y-yeah, sure," I stammered kind of lamely. I hated to admit it, but I did kinda like the guy. I liked the way he put his arm around me, the way he watched me with such intensity, the way his finger had felt pressed against my lips . . . all the things he didn't truly mean— well, I liked them and wished that he did mean them.

"There!" Mama Ling proclaimed as if she'd just unveiled a classic painting.

Opening my eyes, I met my reflection in the mirror. Then I opened them wider, unable to believe what I was seeing. This was me?

With my new contacts I hardly recognized myself. I hadn't planned to wear them, but they were sort of liberating, so I'd decided to go with them. Mama Ling had applied the barest bit of makeup, but it looked so right!

I wore a red dress that gathered at my waist. Pleats flowed through the skirt, and the upper portion greatly resembled a halter. It just left my shoulders bare but not my back. The shade really accented my dark coloring.

"Wow," I breathed in disbelief. I couldn't wait for Nick to see me.

Whoa! Back up that thought. Adam. I wanted

Adam to see me. I wondered if he'd be at the dance. If he was, surely he'd notice me now.

When the doorbell rang, heralding Nick's arrival, my heart thumped and my breath grew shallow. I knew it wasn't the date. It was simply completing an idiotic deal that I'd made with the guy.

Still, I couldn't help but wonder what he'd think.

I opened the door, expecting some sort of flippant, "What, no green gunk?"

Instead I got nothing.

Absolutely nothing. No comment. No, "Hi." No, "Let's go."

Nick just stared at me like he couldn't believe what he was seeing. His gaze traveled slowly from the top of my head to the tips of my shoes, where my toes were peering out—provocatively, if I did say so myself—through the opening in my slingback heels. Then he finally said what I'd said hours ago.

"Wow," but his voice sounded almost hoarse. Then he lifted his eyes to mine. "Wow."

A little thrill shot through me. For a guy who was always charming the girls, he seemed a bit tongue-tied.

Who would have ever thought that I, Edie the Nerd, would silence Nick the Cool?

Not that I was doing much better in the conversation department. Nick looked totally hot.

He wasn't dressed that much differently from his usual black—a satiny shirt in place of the cotton T-shirt—but still he "looked" different. More polished. More cool.

So totally not for me. I had learned long ago to accept who I was, but suddenly, tonight, I was wishing that I was a girl Nick might ask out for real.

Twelve

Nick

Tell one person a secret and you tell the world.
—Mama Ling

I WAS TOTALLY floored when I saw Edie. Man.
She didn't have her glasses on and she was wearing makeup and a red dress that made her look like a Christmas present that I wanted to unwrap way before Christmas morning.

I could hardly take my eyes off her as I drove us to the school. I mean, I'd begun to notice that she was cute . . . in a quirky kind of way. But this Edie was dazzling . . . in a *hot* kind of way.

Ah, man, I was actually wishing that she wasn't going to the dance with me because of the lame excuse I'd given her about wanting to date a brain . . . and because she was fulfilling her end of our deal. I wanted her to be sitting in the car beside me because I, Nick Adriano, had asked her to the dance and she *wanted* to be with *me*.

I was more convinced than ever that nerd boy did not deserve her adoration.

I smoothly pulled the car into a slot. "Wait there," I ordered. Then I hopped out and gave myself a mental shake to slow down. Way down. No need to rush through the evening. Still, I couldn't wait for the guys to see her. She was going to absolutely blow them away.

I opened her door, and she gave me this smile that said, "Thank you," better than any words ever could. It was like we were in sync. I knew what she thought without her having to tell me.

I helped her out of the car, slammed the door shut, and started to sling my arm around her shoulders—something I always did with the babes—but it suddenly didn't seem right to do that with Edie. I cared about her with her usually quirky clothes, the way she constantly blushed.

With Edie, I did something that I'd never done before. I slipped my hand around hers, and somehow with our palms touching, it seemed so much more intimate than having my arm around her. She tilted her head slightly and gave me this shy kinda smile.

And I couldn't remember ever dating a girl who appealed to me more than Edie did at that moment.

"Did Mama Ling happen to give you a fortune for the night?" I asked as we walked toward the gym, where the dance was to be held.

Edie smiled sweetly and blushed. "I don't remember the exact wording, but it was something along the lines of, 'Follow your heart until it leads you to your dreams.'" She shrugged as if embarrassed. "She can get sappy sometimes."

And her dream was to be with Adam. Man, that thought actually brought me down. "Look, Edie, about Adam—I will uphold my end of the bargain."

She shook her head, her hair skimming over her bare shoulders. "You tried, Nick. That's what's important. Tonight I don't want to think about our deal. I just want to enjoy my first dance."

Ah, man, my stomach knotted up. "Your first dance?"

She nodded. "My first date, actually." Then her cheeks flamed red. "Even though I know it's not really a date. It's not like you wanted to bring *me* specifically. You wanted to bring a brain."

"Right," I murmured, wondering why I hadn't seen until now that I did want to bring Edie, Edie the babe, not the brain.

"Now you have to prove you can show me a good time," she teased, a twinkle in her eyes.

"That sounded almost like a dare," I challenged.

"Thought you were daring yourself," she retorted.

"You're right. I think I know exactly how to show you a good time," I said cockily.

She laughed at that, that quiet, tinkling sound that seemed to echo through my chest whenever she made it. I gripped her hand more tightly as we walked into the gym. Or what used to be the gym. Now it was the dance committee's version of a tropical paradise. Muted lights, plastic palm trees.

"This is really bad," I whispered to Edie as we wormed our way through the crowd.

"Hey, Nick!" someone shouted.

Since I didn't recognize the voice, I just gave a brisk nod.

"I think it's wonderful," Edie replied in that optimistic way of hers.

But then, she didn't have a past prom to compare this event to. I found myself hoping she'd have a future prom in the spring. That nerd boy would come to his senses. If he didn't . . . I might just be tempted to bring her. If she got excited over this display of bad design, she'd be euphoric at the prom.

"Nick, looking good, dude," someone said as we passed. I lifted my fist.

"Listen, Edie—"

"Hey, dude," some guy said, slapping my shoulder as he walked by.

"Charlie. Edie, I—"

"Nick, man, what's happening?" Rick Moore asked as he stopped in front of me, but his eyes were glued to Edie. Even though I could see that he was totally absorbed with her, I was irritated.

"What usually happens at a dance," I muttered as I elbowed past him, Edie in tow. "People dance."

With an exaggerated sigh of relief I got Edie onto the dance floor with only about six other people calling out my name. I took her in my arms. Ah, man, did she feel good. And she was wearing this huge smile as she leaned back and looked up at me.

"I never realized being popular was such a burden," she teased.

"Few people do," I said as seriously as I could. "But you gotta please the masses."

She wrinkled her nose. "You love it! Being the center of attention."

"Usually," I admitted. "But tonight I just want to please you."

She gave me that winning smile of hers. "That's a great first step toward showing a brainiac a good time."

I shook my head. "No, Edie, I don't want to show a brain a good time. I want to show Edie Dalton a good time."

Of all the things I'd ever said to Edie, that one was the truest. I wanted *her* to have a good time.

I had to admit that anytime I went on a date, I always thought about having a good time. I thought about me enjoying myself, me having fun, and I always figured if I was happy, then the girl I was with had to be happy as well. Now I wasn't so sure. My reasoning seemed kinda shallow.

For the first time in my life I was thinking as long as the babe I was with had a good time, enjoyed herself, then I knew that I'd have a good time. I wasn't even sure if any of this made sense. I only knew that it was true.

I drew Edie closer until her head could fit into the crook of my shoulder. Her hands rested lightly on my shoulders. She had such small hands. My hands were cupped around her waist. Her tiny waist. Her dress was so satiny, and I figured her skin probably felt the same way. I could feel its warmth seeping through the material.

"I didn't expect dancing to be so easy," she said, almost too quietly for me to hear, as if she were slipping into a dream.

Man, her first dance. "You're a natural," I murmured near her ear.

"Who would have thought I would be?" she commented as if it had never crossed her mind.

"I bet you're a natural at a lot of things," I whispered.

She tilted back her head. "Like what?"

Her eyes were such a deep brown. And her lips. Curved into that quirky smile. I just couldn't get over how kissable they looked. Kissing girls in public places was something that I did with regularity. It was cool not to worry about what people thought.

This dare was all about proving I was cool enough not to care what anyone thought. And what better way to prove my point than with this . . .

I lowered my mouth to hers. I heard her sharp intake of breath. Her fingers dug into my shoulders as if she needed to anchor herself to earth. Her lips were incredibly warm, amazingly soft. I kept moving my feet, just a slight swaying in time to the music so we were dancing and kissing.

I lifted my hand, cupped her cheek, and stroked my thumb over it. It was like satin. Her fingers began to relax, and then she wound her arms around my neck, if at all possible easing her body a little closer to mine.

Fire shot through me. I couldn't count the number of girls I'd kissed, but never before had I felt like the girl was kissing me as well. I should have expected it of Edie. Edie the do-gooder, who took care of stray dogs and hassled friends.

Edie was a giver. She'd never take a kiss without returning it. And she returned it with amazing skill. If I hadn't known it was her first kiss, I never would have guessed.

I drew back and smiled down at her glazed-over eyes and her swollen lips. "Like that," I finally responded to the question she'd asked aeons ago.

Three dances and at least that many kisses later, Edie announced that she needed a break to go to the ladies' room. I offered to amble over to the refreshment table to get us some punch.

She gave me a smile that told me I definitely knew how to show a brainiac a good time. More important, I was actually showing Edie a good time.

I ladled some punch into a plastic cup. Even I was enjoying myself. When the guys had issued the dare and I had accepted, I had immediately drawn certain expectations about this evening. I'd be bored, dancing with every girl except the one I'd brought and watching the seconds tick by like a condemned man waiting for a reprieve.

Instead I'd only danced with Edie. Only wanted

to dance with Edie. I was enjoying myself, and I couldn't believe how quickly the time was flying by. At midnight the dance would come to a close, the dare would be fulfilled, and my time with Edie would end.

Strangely enough, I didn't want to hear the clock strike twelve.

"Hey, Nick!" Jared slapped me on the back.

With Edie's cup of punch in my hand, I turned and faced him and Steve. "Hey, guys."

"Nice show," Steve complimented me.

Huh? I had no idea what he was referring to. "What show?"

"The kisses. You're going above and beyond the limits of the dare," he explained.

Ah, the kisses. They weren't above and beyond anything. They were simply incredible. Just like Edie. But the guys obviously thought I was putting on a show out there. I thought about confessing that Edie's kisses were unlike any I'd before experienced, but even though these were my best buds, there were some things I just couldn't share with them.

"So, you dudes having fun?" I asked.

"Not as much as we thought we'd have," Jared told me. "That show you're putting on doesn't make up for the fact that you didn't uphold your end of the dare."

Okay, I was quickly getting lost here. "What are you talking about?"

"You were supposed to bring a geek to the dance," Jared reminded me. "Bowwow. Woof! Woof!"

Sometimes Jared was totally immature. I had lived up to my end of the dare. "Heh, I brought the girl you guys dared me to bring."

"But giving her a makeover was not part of the dare," Steve announced. "You were supposed to prove that you don't care what people think. Giving her a makeover proves that you absolutely do care."

I held up my hand. "Hey, guys, I didn't give her a makeover. Believe me, I'm as surprised by how hot Edie looks tonight as you are." I considered admitting that it wasn't only her looks that surprised me, but everything else about her as well—her smiles, her laughter, her sense of humor, her intelligence. Yep, I was attracted to her smarts too. But I knew it would be totally uncool to admit any of that to these guys. I had to remain cool at all costs.

The guys were shaking their heads, looking doubtful that I had proved anything. And I knew how they'd razz me if they perceived that I'd wussed out on the dare.

"Believe me, guys, even though Edie has changed on the outside, even though she looks totally hot, she's still the same on the inside—an absolute nerd," I lied, desperate to save face here. "So I fulfilled all the conditions of the dare."

I heard a startled gasp. Dreading what I might find, I spun around and discovered Edie standing there.

And judging by the devastated look on her face, I knew she'd heard everything.

Thirteen

Edie

Tears flow not from the eyes, but from the heart.
—*Mama Ling*

WITH MY HEART pounding, my face flushed with humiliation, I rushed out to the parking lot. I needed to get home. I wanted to hide, but I didn't know where to go or what to do.

Neither Courtney nor Sebastian had come to the dance, so I couldn't turn to them for help. I was totally on my own. I hadn't wanted to be burdened with a purse, so I didn't have any change handy with which to make a call home. I considered dialing 911. After all, I felt sorta like I was dying here. Like my heart was shriveling up, and my chest ached so badly that I could barely breathe. But the arrival of an ambulance would bring attention to me that I absolutely didn't want. It was bad enough that Nick had brought attention my way.

So the only option that remained was using my two legs.

I could walk. It might take hours, but I didn't care as I headed out across the parking lot. I heard feet pounding the pavement behind me.

"Hey, Edie! Wait up!"

Nick. Nick, who I'd actually begun to like. I pressed my hand to my mouth. Oh gosh, I'd let him kiss me. And not just once. During every dance. And worse. Not only had I let him kiss me, but I'd kissed him back! With enthusiasm, with happiness, with joy. How could I have been such a fool? So blind!

He grabbed my arm, and I wrenched free. "Don't touch me. Don't you ever touch me again!"

He held out his hands. "Edie, look, I'm really sorry."

"I don't want to hear it! I couldn't figure out why the coolest guy at Kennedy High would want to go to the dance with the nerdiest girl—"

"Edie, you're not—"

"Don't talk to me!" I shouted. I'd never in my life hurt this badly. Not when I was nine and my gerbil died. Not when I had my tonsils out. "You lied to me about wanting to date a smart girl. I heard everything you and your *friends* were discussing. You were on a dare the entire time! It was all for *show!*"

He took a step toward me. "Edie, I can explain—"

I tapped my temple. "I'm a brain, Nick. I don't need things spelled out. I'm really good at putting two and two together. I'm really skilled at solving complex problems. But this little situation here"—I swung my arm out into a wide arc—"there's nothing complicated about it. It's so incredibly simple. I thought you were something special. Really cool. Instead you're a jerk. Totally and completely."

"Listen, it's not that simple. If you'd just hear me out," he pleaded.

"Do I look like I got stupid all of a sudden?" I asked, knowing I'd been stupid all along. Courtney and Sebastian had both tried to warn me. "Since you seem to like dares so much, I dare you to take me home without saying a word!"

"Edie—"

"Not a word. Just take me home in silence. I *dare* you!"

He nodded somberly as if he'd hit a brick wall that he couldn't knock down. I'd thought he was determined when he kept asking me to the dance. He was just desperate.

Our footsteps echoed so loudly over the parking lot as we walked to the car. I couldn't even bear to look at him as he unlocked the door for me and opened it.

I slid onto the seat. The car smelled so much like him that my stomach roiled and I thought I might be sick.

He climbed behind the steering wheel and started the car. I stared out the window as we rolled away from the school and he turned the vehicle onto the street.

I tried not to humiliate myself any further by crying, but as the streetlights created shifting shadows within the car, I couldn't stop the tears from leaking out of my eyes. Had I actually anticipated tonight? What a fool I'd been.

I thought of all the long, lingering looks he'd given me and how I'd begun to wonder if he was seeing below the surface. I remembered holding his gaze in the hallway. I remembered wishing that he'd been asking me out for real. That hurt worst of all.

Adam as my main crush had begun to dim, and Nick had started to take his place. Nick, who had gouged my heart in his typical self-centered way.

I felt a slight nudge on my arm. Glaring, I jerked around. Nick, with his eyes focused totally on the road, was extending me a tissue box. I didn't want to take it, but I knew my family would be waiting up, and the rivulets running down my face were becoming too much to swipe away with my hand.

"Thanks," I croaked as I snatched it from him and turned away. I wish I hadn't said anything, but manners had been drilled into me. I wanted to curl into a ball to fight off the pain of his betrayal. "Was the whole *cool* clique in on your cruel dare?"

"No. Just me and my buds," he said quietly.

"Some friends you've got. I'd hate to meet your enemies," I rasped, loathing the way the tears burning my throat made me sound sick. But then, I did feel ill.

He brought the car to a halt in front of my house. I heard him shift on the seat, but I didn't wait. I threw open the door, tossed the tissue box onto the seat, and raced up the walk.

I burst through the door and slammed it behind me. I stood there, breathing heavily, my back pressed to the door.

Long minutes passed before I heard the jerk drive away.

Mama Ling was the first one to venture into the foyer.

"Edie, why are you crying?" she asked.

I couldn't tell her the truth: that I had just experienced the most awful, humiliating night of my life. She had been so excited about my first date.

"Tears of joy," I whispered. "I'll tell you all about it in the morning. Right now I just want to go to bed and hold this night close."

Upstairs in my room, I considered crawling onto my bed, curling into a ball, and crying my heart out. But I wouldn't give Nick Adriano the satisfaction of reducing me to that state of despair.

Besides, Mama Ling had taught me well how to relax, how to deal with a crisis, how to rise above grief.

I went into my bathroom and turned on the faucet to the bathtub. Then I poured in half a bottle of bubble bath. I watched the bubbles mount up, one after another. When they reached the rim, I turned off the water. Then I lit the scented candles Mama Ling had given me for Christmas.

I turned out the lights and watched the shadows

dance around the room—slowly, provocatively, just as I'd danced with Nick. Maybe this wasn't such a good idea. But it was too late to turn back.

I pinned my hair on top of my head. As I removed the red dress, I tried not to think about how I'd bought it specifically for this occasion—wanting to please Nick. I growled as I rolled it up into a tight ball. What a fool I'd been.

I removed the remainder of my clothes and got into the tub. I sank down until the water lapped at my throat and the bubbles tickled my chin.

I dipped a washcloth into the water and used it to scrub my mouth, to scrub away any evidence that Nick had ever placed his lips against mine.

Oh my gosh, his kisses had been so incredible. He kissed the way he walked, slowly, tantalizingly. It had felt so real. As if he really meant it, as if he enjoyed it.

Had that been part of the dare as well? Kiss a nerd on the dance floor in front of everyone? Had any of tonight been real? Had any of the past week not been part of the dare?

His smile of appreciation? His help with Adam?

My tears began to fall in earnest, bursting the bubbles that surrounded me.

I was devastated, totally and completely. Nothing about my friendship with Nick had been real.

To Nick Adriano, I had just been a dare.

Fourteen

Nick

It takes much work to right a wrong.
—*Mama Ling*

I SAT IN the darkened living room, staring at images flashing on the muted television.

I couldn't believe how wrong everything had turned out. Or how much of a jerk I was. Almost as much of a jerk as the two guys I called friends. Guys who had laughed—actually laughed—at the sight of Edie's devastated-looking face. I'd wanted to punch them, but I was more concerned about her, so I'd gone after her and left the two bozos to snicker like idiots.

After I'd put my face in theirs and threatened them that if they told one single person, breathed one word of the dare to anyone, I'd make their lives a living hell. "This isn't a dare, guys," I'd vowed. "It's a fact."

I really cared for Edie. That hadn't been part of the dare, but it was what had happened. I had fallen for her. Hard. Like skating for the first time, losing your balance, and landing flat on your butt on the concrete. And I absolutely hated that I had hurt her. Just to save face with the guys.

What was I thinking, to feel like I had to impress them? The whole point of the dare had been to show that I didn't care what people thought—but when it came right down to the wire . . . I had cared. I'd cared enough to lie. I'd cared enough about what they thought *not* to say, "You know, I discovered Edie is an amazing girl. She's funny, witty, smart, caring. She's way cooler than any of us."

But I'd lied and told them she was a nerd on the inside when in truth, I'd been standing there talking to the two biggest nerds I knew. As for myself, I wasn't a nerd. I was an A1 jerk.

"Nick, you okay?" my dad asked from the doorway.

I stopped my mental flaying long enough to say, "Yeah, sure." If realizing that you weren't cool was okay. If your hand being closed around a tissue dampened by a sweet girl's tears was okay.

He sat on the couch beside me. "I assume the geek dare didn't work out too well," he said quietly.

"Ah, Dad," I moaned. "It, like, got totally weird."

"In what way?" he prodded.

"I actually started to like the girl. A lot. More

than a lot. But she heard about the dare, and now she hates me."

"Sounds like you're on your way to figuring it out," he commented.

It? What in the heck was *it?* I hadn't figured anything out except that I was a jerk and Edie didn't deserve to be part of any dare.

"I don't think so, Dad. I always thought I was so cool, and now I'm not even sure that I know what cool is anymore."

"I think you know," he told me. "If you're really a cool guy, you'll know what to do." He patted my shoulder. "You'll know, Nick."

He stood, looking at me like he was searching for the cool guy who no longer existed. "You'll know," he said one last time before going to bed.

I didn't know anything . . . except that I wanted Edie to be happy.

Sunday afternoon, I went to Disk Us. I walked through the store to the computer section. Although walking was too wild a word for the way that I covered ground, with my feet dragging, my shoulders slumped, and my head bent.

Adam spotted me. His face lit up with dollar signs flashing in his eyes as he headed toward me. "So did you decide to get the computer?" he asked when he got near enough.

"Not exactly," I replied.

"You want to look at another model?" he inquired.

"No, I'm not here to buy anything. I'm here to sell you on something."

Then I confessed the details of the whole sordid story. I told him about the dare. How Steve and Jared had selected Edie as the geek I'd take to the dance . . . only she wasn't a geek. But she hadn't wanted to go with me. How she was crushing on Adam, who never noticed her, so I struck a bargain with her. Go with me and I'd get Adam to not only notice her, but ask her out. I even went so far as to tell him about the fiasco at the dance.

The more I talked, the lower his jaw dropped.

By the time I was finished with the amazingly cruel tale, he was looking at me like I was something to be scraped off a shoe. Definitely no longer the coolest guy at Kennedy High.

"You are a total jerk," he announced.

"Yeah, I finally figured that out, but I want to make things right for Edie. I don't know why you never noticed her before. I mean, she's smart, and funny, and kind. She does volunteer work at the animal shelter. The dogs love her." I loved her. Man, where had that thought come from? But it was true. I liked her so much. "She's loyal to her friends. And cute. Adam, she's so cute. She's got this smile. It's kinda quirky, I can't really describe it, but the first time you see it, dude, you're gonna be so glad that you made her smile." I released a deep breath. "So if you think Edie is as awesome as I do, I suggest you ask her out and just forget about all the stupid stuff I tried to pull, okay?"

Adam eyed me suspiciously. "Why would I want to take out any girl who was interested in you?"

This part was difficult to admit, but I'd finally figured out that I would do anything for Edie. "I assure you that Edie has no interest in me whatsoever. She never did. That's the reason I had to strike a bargain with her."

"I saw the way she looked at you," he argued. "Like she practically had stars in her eyes."

Could that be possible? Could Edie have started to care about me the way I did about her? Even if that were true, what chance did I have now? I'd totally blown it.

"Don't say anything about this to Edie, okay?" I pleaded. Even if he decided to ask her out, I didn't want her to know it was because I'd convinced the guy.

"I won't," he promised.

So maybe the guy was cooler than I thought.

At school on Monday my heart was hammering as I walked down the hallway. Guys called out to me, but I barely noticed. None of them had anything to say that I really wanted to hear.

I'd definitely come to a fork in the road, as Mama Ling had predicted. And somehow I'd stumbled on the path that led to misery when I'd been so certain I'd always choose the one that led to happiness. How had I managed to lose Nick Adriano so completely?

Did anyone know Nick? I sure as heck didn't. I

used to strut down the halls with a litany of, "I'm cool. I'm cool," running through my mind as if I needed to convince myself as much as I did everyone else. But when it came right down to it, I wasn't cool at all. I was just a guy looking for acceptance. So afraid if people knew the real Nick, they'd think I wasn't cool.

And *that* was so not cool.

The sweetest girl at Kennedy High had graced my life for a week, and how had I repaid her gift? By humiliating her.

I picked up my pace as I headed down the hallway. I had so many things that I needed to say to Edie. Apologize first, second, and third. Then tell her how wonderful I thought she was. Then confess that I didn't know how to get Adam to ask her out.

My heart rammed against my ribs as I approached her, and my stomach knotted up so tightly that I wasn't certain if I'd ever be able to eat. "Hey, Edie—"

She slammed her locker closed and glared at me. "I dare you not to speak to me for the rest of my life."

I watched her trudge away. It was hard to be cool when your heart was hurting.

Fifteen

Edie

To touch a dream, you must hold out your hand.
                                    —*Mama Ling*

I SAT IN the cafeteria with Courtney and Sebastian. Sebastian hadn't even said he told me so; that was what a best friend he was.

I had been hoping, wanting Nick to be my friend. Someone I could share things with. Someone I wanted to date. Boy, was I wrong there.

I had nothing but bad memories of the dance. I had absolutely no desire to be a friend or acquaintance of Nick's.

Sebastian and Courtney were being extra nice to me, even though I actually had hung out with that jerk Nick for a while.

"Did you notice the way Adam was watching

you today in the hallway while you were putting your books in your locker?" Courtney asked.

"Yeah," I mumbled, studying the flat, pointed object that the cafeteria menu had labeled as pizza. The worst part of this whole scenario was that Adam *had* finally noticed me and probably thought I was the biggest idiot at Kennedy High. I sure felt like an idiot. Just like every girl at Kennedy, once Nick flashed that grin her way, her IQ dropped fifty points. Only mine had dropped about a hundred.

"I saw him nod with admiration when you told Nick off when he stopped at your locker," Sebastian offered, trying to give me hope that my world wasn't as bleak as I thought it was.

"I'm sure he was approving of something else," I muttered. Probably the way Nick strutted down the hallway.

"I like your contacts," he blurted.

That made me smile at him. He was trying so hard to lift my spirits. I had decided that I liked the contacts after all. "Thanks, Sebastian. I'm thinking of getting my tongue pierced next."

"No way!" he and Courtney cried at the same time.

And I laughed. "I figure if I can put something in my eye, I can put a piece of metal through my tongue."

We all three shivered at the same time. Courtney rubbed her ear. "Ear piercing was enough for me." She leaned forward. "You know what I don't understand?"

"Calculus?" I asked.

She grinned. "No, I've got that down. What I don't understand is why I haven't heard anything about this stupid dare from anyone except you."

She had a point. I'd really dreaded coming to school this morning. I had expected people to whisper behind my back, point fingers. Say to my face, "Could you get any stupider?"

"I mean, when Nick asked you to the dance during lunch, I heard about it before I got to fourth period. But this . . . Edie, the school should have been buzzing about this dare. There wasn't even anything about it on Nick's Web site," she told me.

My mouth dropped open. "You went to the official Nick Adriano Web site?"

Courtney's cheeks turned red. "Well, yeah. I just wanted to know what they were saying out there." She scrunched up her face. "They posted a picture of you dancing with Nick."

I grimaced. "What did I look like?"

"Like you thought he was really cool."

"Well, he's not," I assured her. "I had a serious lapse in judgment for a few days, but as Mama Ling would say, 'Experience is the best teacher,' and I learned that if I can't figure out why a guy is paying attention to me, there's probably a reason."

Suddenly Jared and Steve dropped down on either side of Sebastian. They kinda squeezed against him until his shoulders were hunched up to his ears.

"Hand it over," Jared ordered in a threatening voice.

Out of the corner of my eye I saw Nick saunter-ing over in that lazy way of his, like he expected life to just wait for his arrival. My heart twisted into a painful knot.

"What's going on, guys?" he asked casually.

My heart nearly shattered. It was so obvious that these guys were hassling Sebastian, and Nick must have seen nothing wrong with it to stand there looking so cool, like he didn't have a care in the world.

How could I have been so blind about Nick? He was as big a jerk as his friends. Why had I over-looked that? Had I wanted to hang around him and see if he'd rub off on me, just a little?

Did I want to be this uncaring, this selfish, this self-centered? Nick Adriano thought the world re-volved around him.

"I want the shrimp's chemistry homework," Jared snarled. "Right now!"

"Leave him alone," Nick and I demanded at the same time.

I snapped my gaze to his. Somehow he didn't look like the same Nick that I'd spent the last week with. He looked, I don't know, lonely. Sad, even. He had dark circles under his eyes, like maybe he wasn't sleeping so well.

Nick wrapped his hand around Jared's arm and yanked him to his feet until they were standing toe to toe, eye to eye. "Do your own damn home-work," Nick said in a low voice that I thought sounded more threatening than anything Jared had ever said to Sebastian. "If I catch you bothering Sebastian again, you're gonna have to deal with me. Trust me on this, dude, you don't want that."

Jared shrugged. "Whatever, man."

"You're sure issuing a lot of ultimatums lately on how we have to act," Steve challenged.

"You don't like it, dude," Nick responded flatly, "hang out with someone else."

Steve looked like a little kid who'd just had someone snatch his lollipop out of his hand. "I meant no offense, man. We can leave the shrimp alone, we can keep our mouths shut about the dance dare. No problem."

"Then let's go," Nick ordered, but he still had that edge to his voice. He led the way out with Jared and Steve trotting along like the dogs at the shelter.

Sebastian and Courtney were staring at each other as if each expected the other to explain what had just happened.

Courtney looked at me. "Someone feels bad about what happened Saturday night."

At least I knew now why no one at school seemed to realize that my going to the dance with Nick had been a dare, not a date.

"It was kind of rude of him not to say anything to you," Courtney admonished.

"I dared him not to speak to me for the rest of my life," I told her.

"Just be careful," Sebastian added. "I'm not sure I trust him just because he saved my homework."

"Not a problem," I told them. "I don't trust him, and I never will again." Not with my heart.

Chemistry, history, English . . .

Walking to my locker, I was ticking off all the classes in which I had homework. Normally I looked forward to the challenge of writing a paper or memorizing facts. Tonight I planned to use every subject as an escape.

I planned to drown myself in homework, as it were. Become so lost in it that maybe I would forget about Nick and, more, the pain he'd caused me.

Nick. He'd seemed so genuinely interested in the things I had to say. I enjoyed studying, but I couldn't say that I really had fun with it. Being with Nick had been fun. Even if in the end it wasn't so cool. For a while I'd felt connected. As lame as it sounded, I thought we were some sort of kindred spirits. In my heart of hearts I think I'd actually been harboring the hope that he cared for me as much as I had begun to care for him.

I'd been a fool in love. I'd fallen for him hook, line, and sinker. He'd tossed out the bait, and all he'd had to do was reel me in.

At my locker I noticed something sticking out from the opening in the door. I was sort of an organization nut, so nothing ever hung out of my locker. I pulled it loose. An envelope.

I opened it up. Inside was an article taken from *Texas Monthly* about the first serial killer in Texas. On a Post-it note was written:

*Ran across this article. Thought you could use it
for your research paper.*
   I'm so sorry, Edie. For everything.
             Nick

Ran across it? Not likely, I realized. Nick "studying is so lame" Adriano would have only run across it if he'd been purposely searching for it. A bouquet of flowers wouldn't have touched me more.

"Hi, Edie."

Adam! I twisted around, and there stood the guy that I'd been crushing on for over a year. He'd actually spoken my name. He was at my locker! Just as I'd dreamed it a hundred times.

So why didn't my heart do that little flip that it usually did? Why was I standing here breathing normally and not anxiously anticipating his next spoken word?

"I really admire all the volunteer work you do for PAL," he enthused.

I furrowed my brow. "How did you know about my volunteer work?"

"Nick mentioned it when he was at the store," Adam explained.

Nick. Yeah, I could imagine the things Nick had told him. Or maybe not. My fingers closed around the article.

"You know, it's funny. We've probably had classes together for years, and I've never really noticed you," he said.

"Yeah, we *have had* classes together," I told him.

"Guess I keep my face buried in the books too much." He shifted his stance.

"I do that as well," I admitted.

"Listen, if you'd like to go out sometime, I'd really like that," he said.

Obviously Nick hadn't given Adam such a bad impression of me if he was willing to ask me out. My heart started doing this boom-boom-boom like the bass drum in the band. But it wasn't because after all this time, my dream had come true. Adam had finally asked me out. My heart was banging against my ribs because I realized that I was no longer interested.

I had another guy on the brain, even if he was a total and complete jerk.

Adam glanced at the tiles between his feet before lifting his gaze to mine. "But I figure I'm too late since I can tell that Nick really likes you."

Ha! That was the joke of the year. Nick was just a great actor.

Still, I knew it wouldn't be fair to Adam to go out with him when I knew I'd be thinking about jerk boy the entire time.

I smiled kindly at Adam. "Yeah, you're too late."

He smiled back. "Understood."

Then the guy who I'd wanted to notice me for so long . . . walked away.

"He who dreams big achieves great things," Mama Ling announced. She smiled as she began to carefully write out the fortune.

I was sitting on a stool at the kitchen counter, helping her. "Why do you always say 'he' in the fortunes? That is so sexist."

She laughed lightly. "Then I will say 'she' for this one and hope that a guy does not open the fortune cookie this one goes in."

I shook my head. "I just don't understand why a female can read a fortune that's talking about what a guy does and realize that it applies to her, but if a guy gets a fortune that mentions a she, he'll get all bent out of shape."

"Because women are more tolerant," she assured me.

"Maybe you need to start doing your fortune cookies in colors, pink and blue," I suggested. "Then you could have specific fortunes for women and men."

"Ah, but Edie, you forget. A person should be able to apply any fortune to his—excuse me—her life." She smiled in that insightful way she had.

"Whatever," I mumbled. "I just don't understand why guys have to have the world cater to their whims."

I began writing some fortunes to share with her. I could think better when writing. "He who is a jerk remains a jerk." For that one I could have actually put the person's name. "She who is a nerd remains a nerd."

The funny thing was, though, I didn't feel so much like a nerd anymore. I mean, there wasn't anything wrong with being smart and studying.

And maybe my clothes weren't always the latest fashion, maybe they were a little quirky even, but I liked them. They were what I was comfortable wearing. Wasn't it better to be comfortable in your clothes than wondering if you looked like everyone else?

Granted, I wasn't popular like Nick. At the dance everyone had spoken to him. I furrowed my brow. No, I thought. They hadn't spoken to him. They'd *greeted* him. A major difference there. The more I thought about it, the more I realized that except for his pals, Mutt and Jeff, I'd never seen Nick actually talk to anyone.

He'd talked to me, made me feel special when I wasn't.

"She who wears a frown is deeply troubled," Mama Ling interrupted my thoughts.

Meeting her gaze, I took a deep breath. "The dance was awful."

"What was so bad?" she prodded gently.

"Nick. Oh, Mama Ling, he was using me. He had accepted this stupid dare to take a 'geek' to the dance. I was the geek."

She wrapped her arms around me and began to rock me gently. "No, no, Edie. You are not a geek. You are a lovely young woman. This Nick . . . he is the geek. He is just a dumb mutt."

I worked my way out of her embrace. "Mutts aren't dumb."

I remembered how I'd explained that to Nick and how I'd teased him about the girl dog being smarter than he was. He hadn't been offended. As a matter of fact, I'd thought I'd seen admiration in his eyes.

"Are eyes like fortune cookies?" I asked her. "When you look in someone's eyes, does what you see there apply to everyone?"

"Oh no, Edie. The eyes are very specific. Why?" she asked.

I kinda shrugged. "Sometimes I thought it looked like maybe Nick admired me. Liked me, even. A lot. But that makes no sense. If he liked me, then why did he tell the guys that I was a nerd? How could he like a nerd?"

"Sometimes a heart must lose its way before it can find the right path to follow," she mused.

I shook my head. "I don't think he lost his heart." But I'd certainly lost mine. "I know I should hate him, Mama Ling, but the truth is that I think I really fell for Nick."

Sixteen

Nick

A true friend always forgives.
—*Mama Ling*

IWAS FEELING totally, completely uncool as I mucked dog poop out of the kennels at the animal shelter.

It was sort of a rite of passage that new volunteers had to go through. I had tried to get Jared and Steve to come, but they wouldn't deal. As a matter of fact, they'd kinda looked at me as if I'd sprouted alien antennae out of the top of my head.

They weren't totally bad guys. Besides, I figured I could be a good influence on them, eventually, now that I had figured out some stuff. Like being cool had nothing to do with the way you walked or dressed or talked. Being cool, as lame as it sounded, had to do with what was inside a person. Actions, not accessories.

My thinking was definitely getting too heavy here. But what else was there to do as I collected these droppings?

I figured Mr. Logon was testing my dedication to the cause of lost or abandoned animals. I crouched down to scoop the latest collection of disgusting stuff onto the pan.

A tiny white fur ball bounded over and licked my hand like she knew I could use a friend. "Hey, Yippy. Edie told me that mutts weren't dumb, so what are you doing hanging around me, huh?"

She rose up on her hind legs and put her paws on my knees. I rubbed her head. "You're a cute little thing, you know that?"

She tossed her head and barked like she thought she was as tough as any of the bigger dogs in the kennel. I picked her up. She was so little that she could sit in my cupped hands. "You are so not cool."

She licked my wrist and squirmed, her little rear end keeping pace with her wagging tail as she barked some more. "You want to go home with me?"

She started panting. I thought maybe she was actually smiling. "But I'm not going to fall for you, not the way I fell for Edie. I can tell you that right now. You're not going to wrap me around your little paw. No, sirree."

But the truth was, she already had. The dumb mutt.

"Looking for another *geek* to date?"

My stomach dropped to the ground. Edie. I'd specifically selected Wednesday as my volunteer day so our paths wouldn't cross. It hurt to see her across the hall at school. I really didn't want to see her close-up, to be reminded of what I might have had if I hadn't turned out to be such a world-class jerk.

Slowly I put Yippy down, stood, and twisted around. "I thought you did your volunteer work on Tuesday."

She shrugged those tiny shoulders of hers. "When I'm feeling down, I like to come here to work."

My chest tightened. She didn't have to tell me that I was the reason she was feeling down. Honestly, the last thing that I had wanted to do was hurt her, but how did I explain that to her? More, how did I convince her to believe me? I'd sort of blown my credibility with her.

"So what are you doing here?" she wanted to know.

"Just had some free time and thought I'd put it to good use." The truth was, although I'd never confess it, I'd sorta been evaluating myself lately, and I wasn't real happy with what I saw. I'd gotten so caught up in worrying about what other people thought of me that I'd forgotten what mattered most was what I thought of me.

Her mouth kinda twitched, and I thought maybe she was going to forgive me.

She nodded down toward the ground. "You stepped in the poop."

I lifted my foot and glared at my shoe. "Ah, sh—" I stopped and jerked my gaze to hers.

She did smile then. "Exactly."

Yippy started yapping.

"You probably want to take the mutt for a walk," she suggested, and turned to go. She stopped and glanced over her shoulder. "Thanks for helping Sebastian."

"No problem. I should have done it before."

Her smile softened then. "Yeah, you should have."

As I watched her walk away, I thought there were a lot of things I should have done. Like not falling for Edie.

Friday night I was at Pizza Pie with Jared and Steve. Lauren, Megan, and Angela had joined us.

We were sharing a pizza laden with everything under the sun and a pitcher of root beer.

"Nick, you looked so good at the dance," Angela enthused.

I'd felt anything but good after I'd hurt Edie. Angela and her friends had all wound up with dates to the dance. Beautiful girls usually did. For them it had probably just been another dance, another date.

For Edie everything had been a first. I'd certainly made sure it was an emotional night for her. I remembered how happy she'd looked when I'd simply said, "Wow," when I'd first seen her at the door. She'd been genuinely pleased.

Most girls that I took out acted like they were

deserving of compliments. I handed them out because they were expected, and they thanked me because it was expected. But nothing about the exchange was ever truly appreciated.

Edie had appreciated my reaction.

But I hadn't been content with that. No, sir. I'd wanted her to run the gamut of emotions. From pleasure to devastation. I'd managed that with amazing accuracy.

"I thought Edie looked good," Lauren announced.

"Edie looked *terrific,*" I said quietly. And she had. So totally hot. But then, in truth, she always looked hot . . . if you knew how to look beyond the surface.

"So how come you aren't seeing her anymore?" Megan asked.

I lifted my mug of root beer. "Because I'm not cool enough."

That made the babes laugh, like they thought it was some sort of joke. But it was so far from being a joke that I could only label it as a resounding disappointment.

They started talking about people they'd seen at the dance. How uncool one girl's dress had been. How uncool some guy had danced.

They mentioned someone's shoes, another girl's hair, how so-and-so had broken up with so-and-so. Boring stuff.

I was doing my typical Nick-nodding-like-he-cared routine, and it suddenly hit me hard that not once while I was with Edie had I ever done that. I'd hung on to every word she said. About dumb mutts, her mother's pet compatibility, her theory on Jack the Ripper's vacation in Texas.

Not once in all our time together did I ever hear her put anyone down. Not until the final hour anyway, when my actions had so totally devastated her that she called me a jerk. But even that was a much softer name than I had deserved.

Edie Dalton was a class act.

"Hey," Steve said in a conspiratorial whisper as he leaned toward me. "Look who's here."

I followed his gaze across the crowded restaurant to the arcade nook. Edie.

My heart did this little stammer. She looked happy, with Courtney and Sebastian flanking her while she worked the controls on some video game.

"Dare you to go over there and talk to her," Steve challenged.

I shook my head. "I don't accept dares anymore."

At least not where Edie was concerned.

Seventeen

Edie

Love is a blossoming of the heart.
—*Mama Ling*

I KNEW NICK was watching me long before he stepped into the arcade nook and I saw his reflection in the glass of the video monitor. I always felt his gaze on me. When I wandered the halls at school. When I ate in the cafeteria. Whenever our paths crossed.

I'd dared him not to talk to me for the rest of my life, and I guess he had decided he was going to accept the dare, but that didn't mean he couldn't still look at me.

I was punching buttons, really kicking butt on this video game—whatever game it was. Bad guys kept jumping out from behind boxes, and I had to blast them. I didn't normally slip into the arcade, but Sebastian had challenged Courtney to a game, and so I'd tagged along.

The monitor started flashing, counting down the number of seconds I had remaining in which I could feed the machine more coins or lose my points. I searched my pockets. Nothing.

"Here," Nick said as he crouched beside the machine and slid some coins into the slots.

The bad guys started appearing again, and I started firing.

"You're pretty good," Nick murmured.

"Yep. Using a complex mathematical formula, I'm able to predict where the next bad guy will appear before he does," I said incredibly seriously.

"You're kidding."

I glanced up at him. "Yeah, I am."

He looked like he wasn't sure if it would be okay if he smiled at my lame joke. I couldn't explain why I was so happy that he'd come over here. I didn't really want to analyze my feelings.

I looked past his shoulder. The table he'd been sitting at was empty. "What happened to your friends?"

"They decided to go to a movie," he explained.

"So you just abandoned your date?" I asked.

"No date. The girls asked if they could sit at our table. No one objected."

"Looked like you were having fun." I was punching buttons but not looking at the screen. I was probably getting creamed.

"Looks can be deceiving," he said quietly.

The machine started beeping, wanting me to feed it more coins. I stepped away, and some guy quickly took my place.

"I heard you adopted Yippy," I commented.

His cheeks turned red, and he shrugged like it was no big deal. "The mutt just wouldn't shut up, you know?"

It was hard not to forgive a guy who was willing to provide a home for an abandoned animal. "I think it's cool that you gave her a home."

And then he smiled. Subtly. I couldn't quite explain it, but it seemed like it was the first *real* smile he'd ever given me. Like he was glad that he'd done something that I thought was cool.

"Can we go outside for a minute?" Nick asked. "Where it's not quite so noisy?"

I hesitated. Did I really want to spend time in the company of Nick?

"Please, Edie," he said with such sincerity that I couldn't say no.

"Okay."

We started walking through the restaurant. He shoved his hands into his pockets, and I wondered briefly if it was because he wanted to put his arm around my shoulders or hold my hand. When we got to the door, he pushed it open for me.

Then we stepped onto the terrace, where people ate on warm summer nights. Tonight there were just a couple of people out here.

I faced Nick. The outside lights were bright

enough that I could see him clearly. That gorgeous face that I had carried into my dreams every night even though I didn't want to.

"Edie, I know I hurt you, and I know that you probably hate me—you have every reason to hate me—but I wanted to ask you to forgive me."

I just stood there, my heart beginning to pound.

"Asking you out started as a dare, and I took it because I thought I was above caring what people thought, that I could take a girl who wasn't in my, uh, social circle to the dance. But I learned that I did care what people thought: what *I* thought, what *you* thought." He shifted his stance, his gaze growing more intense. I watched him swallow. "I also learned that I *like* you. Big time. I learned that there's no brain, no cool, no circle; there are just people. I don't know if you'll ever forgive me, but I hope someday that you will."

My heart started hammering. "Did someone dare you to like me, Nick?" I asked.

"No, where you're concerned, Edie, I don't take dares anymore. Ever. You're too special. I know I blew it with you, and I can't tell you how much I regret that."

Nick thought I was special? This warm feeling like melted honey just kinda poured through me.

"And I'm really sorry that I couldn't get you the date with Adam like I promised," he told me with such sincerity.

I smiled then. "But you know what, Nick? You got me something better."

"I did?" he asked, clearly baffled.

I nodded. "You got me a date with a guy I didn't even know I wanted one with. And I'm thinking that maybe we should go on a makeup date and see what happens."

Nick grinned at me in true geek fashion.

Saturday evening I stared at my reflection in the mirror. Where was the nerd?

I'd brushed my hair to a glowing sheen. I wore my new contacts. I'd lightly applied makeup.

I wore a denim dress, and over it I wore a red chenille sweater. I liked layered looks. I was comfortable in clothes that didn't hug my body.

Quite honestly, I was comfortable in my own skin, as some old saying went. I didn't see a nerd in the mirror because . . . I'd never been a nerd to begin with.

Yes, I was a brain. I was fascinated with facts and the challenge of figuring things out. I'd just never figured out that the way you saw yourself could overshadow the way you truly were.

I mean, look at Nick. He thought he was cool. He projected "cool." But when it came right down to it, he hadn't been cool at all. Until recently.

And me, well, I wasn't a nerd. I'd just allowed people to project their prejudices against brainy people on me.

I was, however, nervous. Nick and I were going to have our first "real" date. I no longer counted the dance as anything but an experience. Not even a humiliating experience. I'd trusted Nick, and he'd broken that trust. I could only hope that he wouldn't do that tonight.

Taking a deep breath, I walked out of my room and down the hallway to the kitchen. Mama Ling was carefully writing out a fortune. She glanced up as I walked in. "Oh, Edie, you look so beautiful."

"You always say that," I chided.

She smiled softly. "Because it is always true."

I sat on the stool beside her. "Mama Ling, I'm trying not to be afraid, afraid Nick is going to hurt me again."

She put her hand over mine. "It is hard to build trust. But I think Nick knows that he hurt himself too."

I nodded. "I overheard him tell Yippy that he'd fallen for me." Before that, I hadn't dared to believe Adam's comment about Nick liking me. *Dared?* I really needed to get that word out of my vocabulary.

She furrowed her brow. "Who is Yippy?"

"A pup he adopted." I hated to acknowledge how cute I'd thought it was to watch Nick carry on a conversation with the little mutt. It had sorta made the hardness around my heart soften slightly. Just a bit. Enough to admit that he might be worth giving another chance.

The doorbell rang. I hopped off the stool and ran my fingers through my hair. "Okay. The moment of truth," I muttered.

I walked to the front door and opened it. My

eyes widened, and my mouth dropped open.

"Not cool, huh?" Nick asked.

He was wearing khaki pants and a pale blue shirt. Blue. Not black. The light blue made his dark features look even more mysterious.

I smiled brightly.

He grinned and looked past me. "Hello, Mama Ling."

I turned to see my grandmother standing there, smiling. "Ah, you finally have some color in your life."

Nick took my hand and pulled me toward him. "I hope so."

I should have known that Nick would take me to a Chinese restaurant. It was so very hushed here. Orchids adorned the table, and in the center was a small candle that flickered between us.

The waitress served us quietly, hardly intruding at all.

And Nick, well, Nick was incredibly attentive and sweet. Opening doors for me, pulling out my chair. And listening so intently to everything that I said, as if each word was encased in gold.

"So I couldn't prove Jack the Ripper came to Texas," I admitted with a sigh. "But my gut just tells me that they accused the wrong person."

"Maybe Jack had a cousin. Insanity ran in the family," he suggested.

"I might pursue that angle," I told him. "How's Yippy?"

I was ready to change the subject, and just as Nick had all evening, he accommodated me.

"She's probably sitting in my dad's lap right now, watching television. They seem to have bonded," he told me.

I sipped my tea. "It was really nice of you to adopt her."

He shrugged. "I'm discovering that it's better to be nice than cool."

I shook my head. "You know, Nick, no matter what you do, I think you'll be cool."

He took my hand. "Edie, I wasn't cool where you were concerned. I hate so badly that I hurt you."

"I'm healing, Nick." I glanced around the restaurant. "This atmosphere helps me to relax."

The waitress set a small tray on the table. Two fortune cookies rested on it. In a move uncharacteristic for the evening, Nick snatched them both up. "I want to save them for later."

Holding hands, Nick and I walked slowly toward my house. This evening would be one that I'd never forget. After we'd left the restaurant, he'd taken me to a movie. *All the Pretty Horses.* Who would have ever thought that cool Nick would sit through a chick flick, holding my hand and sharing my popcorn?

I had an incredible feeling that this wouldn't be the last evening that I spent with Nick.

When we got to the door, Nick handed me one of the fortune cookies. The porch light was shining brightly, so I had no trouble seeing the sparkle in his eyes.

I snapped open my cookie and read the fortune. "The coolest thing a guy can do is be crazy about Edie."

With tears stinging my eyes, I slowly brought my gaze to his. "How did you manage this?"

"Your grandmother helped me out. I told her the fortune that I wanted. She wrote it out and put it in a cookie for me." He took a step closer. "I guess you were right all along, Edie. A fortune does apply to everyone . . . if a guy is smart enough to realize that."

"Nick—"

"I'm crazy about you, Edie."

I smiled softly, my heart just sort of unfurling like a flower when the sun touches it. "I dare you to kiss me."

"I've sort of sworn off dares," he whispered. "But I'm smart enough to know when one is worth accepting."

Nick cupped my face between his hands and lowered his mouth to mine. The kiss was just like Nick. So hot. And just like Nick, so cool. Because the truth was, Nick was a complicated guy who could challenge his buds to leave Sebastian alone and then adopt the geekiest-looking dog at the shelter.

I eased my arms up around his neck. He groaned, lowered his arms to my back, and drew me closer as his lips played over mine.

My heart did this little flip—a swan dive off the high board, right into the deepest part of the pool. I was falling for Nick, hard. We had so much to learn about each other, so much to talk about. His family, my family, our friends, our hopes for the rest of high school, college, everything. I couldn't wait to hear everything Nick Adriano had inside him.

Breathing heavily, he leaned back slightly and tucked my hair behind my ear. "So you think there's a future for us?"

"You mean for Nick and the nerd?"

He shook his head. "For Nick and Edie."

I smiled. "Definitely."

He grinned, a warm, sensual smile that I'd never seen him give anyone. Then he kissed me again.

Just as he'd told me last night, there were no labels between us.

Just two hearts beating as one. And that was totally cool.

Do you ever wonder about falling in love? About members of the opposite sex? Do you need a little friendly advice but have no one to turn to? Well, that's where we come in . . . Jenny and Jake. Send us those questions you're dying to ask, and we'll give you the straight scoop on life and love.

DEAR JAKE

Q: *I've been dating my boyfriend for almost a month, and I'm totally crazy about him. Problem is, I'm always the one who initiates our plans, like hooking up at lunch or going to the movies or the mall on the weekends. If I didn't, I feel like I'd never even see him! What should I do?*

KP, Tulsa, OK

A: Hmmm . . . would you really never have *any* plans if you didn't make them? Is he taking you for granted, or are you a bit of a control freak? Perhaps you should test out your theory. Don't make all the plans for the two of you—then wait to see what happens. I'll bet you find him at your locker by the end of the day or on the other end of the phone or instant messaging you to find out what you want to do that night or that weekend. Perhaps you just haven't given the guy a chance to make plans with you. Or perhaps you're right . . . perhaps he's letting you do all the work. There's only one way to find out, and that's to see what happens if you stop taking total control of the relationship. He just might surprise you!

Q: *Every time my boyfriend and I disagree, instead of discussing the problem, he buys me presents. Maybe that sounds sweet, but it drives me crazy—we never get anything solved! Should I just appreciate the nice gestures that he's trying to make, or does this need to change?*

ST, Mandeville, LA

A: Sounds like your guy has some trouble expressing himself verbally and likes making up with gifts. Hey, nothing wrong with getting that CD or sweater you've been saving up for, but you're right: if he expects the gift to take care of the problem, then you do need to work on getting him to open up. Let him know you do appreciate the gesture but that it would really help to talk about the disagreement too. Go slowly.

DEAR JENNY

Q: *Almost every time we go out, my boyfriend and I go to places that he wants to go. Why is it that we do only what he wants to?*

JE, Lincoln, NE

A: Does he say "no way" to the stuff you want to do? If so, you two need to spend your next date having a *major* conversation. Or do you keep quiet about what you'd rather do and just go along with whatever he suggests? Sometimes it's hard to tell a guy you don't want to go to the batting cages or hike up some mountain or play video games with his buds. But if you always go along with what he wants to do, you're not going to have much fun . . . or let him get to know who you are and what you like to do.

Q: *Every time I'm crushing over a guy, I lose interest in him once he likes me back. It just recently happened with a really nice guy, and I feel terrible that my feelings have faded now that he likes me. What can I do about this?*

LR, Brooklyn, NY

A: Well, it sounds like you enjoy chasing a guy more than actually catching him. It might mean that you're not ready for a relationship (afraid, perhaps?), or it might mean that you simply like winning over someone you're crushing on. Thing is, if you've won over someone, then you're dealing with someone else's feelings. And it's not too cool to play around with someone's heart. Next time you find yourself going after a guy, ask yourself if you really like him or if you just want to see if you can get him. If you don't really have feelings for the guy, stop. And go for the guy you really want!

Do you have any questions about love?
Although we can't respond individually to your letters,
you just might find your questions answered in our column.

Write to:
Jenny Burgess or Jake Korman
c/o 17th Street Productions,
an Alloy Online, Inc. company.
151 West 26th Street
New York, NY 10001

Don't miss any of the books in *Love Stories*
—the romantic series from Bantam Books!

SUPER EDITIONS

TRILOGIES

LOVE STORIES: HIS. HERS. THEIRS.

Coming soon:

BFYR 232

You'll always remember your first love.

Love Stories

Looking for signs he's ready to fall in love?

Want the guy's point of view?

Then you should check out *Love Stories*. Romantic stories that tell it like it is—why he doesn't call, how to ask him out, when to say good-bye.

Love Stories
Available wherever books are sold.